D0517359

EAGLE VALLEY LIBRARY DISTRICT
P.O. BOX 240 600 BROADWAY
EAGLE, CO 81631 / 328-8800

BLOWN

Also by Mark Haskell Smith

Fiction

Moist

Delicious

Salty

Baked

Raw: A Love Story

Nonfiction

*Heart of Dankness: Underground Botanists,
Outlaw Farmers, and the Race for the Cannabis Cup*

*Naked at Lunch: A Reluctant Nudist's Adventures in
the Clothing-Optional World*

BLOWN

A NOVEL

MARK HASKELL SMITH

Black Cat
New York

Copyright © 2018 by Mark Haskell Smith

All rights reserved. No part of this book may be reproduced in any form or by any electronic or mechanical means, including information storage and retrieval systems, without permission in writing from the publisher, except by a reviewer, who may quote brief passages in a review. Scanning, uploading, and electronic distribution of this book or the facilitation of such without the permission of the publisher is prohibited. Please purchase only authorized electronic editions, and do not participate in or encourage electronic piracy of copyrighted materials. Your support of the author's rights is appreciated. Any member of educational institutions wishing to photocopy part or all of the work for classroom use, or anthology, should send inquiries to Grove Atlantic, 154 West 14th Street, New York, NY 10011 or permissions@groveatlantic.com.

FIRST EDITION

Published simultaneously in Canada
Printed in the United States of America

This book is set in Garamond Premier by
Alpha Design & Composition in Pittsfield, NH.

First Grove Atlantic paperback edition: June 2018

Library of Congress Cataloging-in-Publication data available for this title.

ISBN 978-0-8021-2814-0
eISBN 978-0-8021-6575-6

Black Cat
an imprint of Grove Atlantic
154 West 14th Street
New York, NY 10011

Distributed by Publishers Group West

groveatlantic.com

18 19 20 21   10 9 8 7 6 5 4 3 2 1

For MacKenzie & Steven; Jon & DLD

BLOWN

AT SEA

Neal Nathanson thought about drinking his own urine. Isn't that what you do when you're out of water? Wasn't that what the Chilean soccer team did when they crashed into the Andes? Or was it the Chilean miners? He was sure someone from Chile had survived some kind of ordeal by drinking piss.

He slumped back on the deck of the wrecked sailboat, lying like a corpse amid the twisted metal and cracked wood, the tangles of rope and cable, feeling the hull bob and roll, powerless against the swell and surge of the open ocean, the horizon bisecting the world into water and sky.

He wiped the salt spray off his glasses with his shirt and put them back on, blinking at the nighttime sky, looking at an infinity of stars and planets and galaxies and supernovas and black holes and red giants and white dwarfs and whatever else was up there. There were way too many, all piled on top of each other, and he didn't recognize a single constellation.

He missed New York City. The traffic, the noise, the light pollution. The universe isn't so vast and oppressive when you can't see it.

Neal knew that ancient mariners had navigated by using the stars, and now that he thought of it, there was probably an app he could have downloaded about marine navigation but there wasn't time. Besides, the boat was state of the art, with a full tech package: there was a backup hard drive for the computer, a streaming weather update, a satellite-guided navigation system with charts and maps, even an emergency distress signal; you could send an email and make phone calls. Of course none of the electronics worked once the seawater got in them.

He had no idea what happened to the sail. Torn off. Sucked into the abyss. Eaten by sea monsters. Who knew? The boat was destroyed. The interior cabin had been cracked like an eggshell, the doors blown off their hinges. Neal was grateful the thing still floated. But where was everyone? Had anyone else survived?

And what happened to Bryan LeBlanc? He started this. It was all his fault.

Neal picked a piece of peeling skin off his sunburnt forehead, rolled it between his fingers, and popped it in his mouth. It tasted salty, like prosciutto. It probably wasn't the smartest thing to do, eating his own dead skin, but he'd been unable to catch a fish or a bird or even a fucking mosquito, and he was starving. Not starving like he used to feel on his way to dinner at some new bistro all the way out in Brooklyn; he was authentically starving, he hadn't eaten in three days, not since he choked down the final chunk of moldy Camembert.

On the positive side, he'd surpassed his weight-loss goal. It was not easy to be upbeat in this situation, but he didn't want to succumb to despair and be one of those guys you read about in the news who gave up and died. It had been easy when there was food on the boat. He'd managed to make it last for over a week, but now he'd gone days without eating anything. Weren't there lots of stories about people adrift for months? How did they survive? He realized that he was experiencing an unhealthy level of anxiety. It felt like a panic attack.

Neal took a deep breath. He needed to be calm. Rational. This current state of affairs called for proactive solutions. He wasn't going to lie there and wait for the seagulls to peck his eyes out. If he had to, if it came down to it, he'd drink a cup of piss.

He rolled onto his belly and slowly pulled himself up. His legs were wobbly and he got dizzy if he stood too fast, so he took his time, using the wheel for balance, making his way into the cabin. The interior, which had once looked like a serene and stylish room in a boutique hotel, now resembled a bedroom after a tornado. Or the inside of a dumpster. He fished an empty wine bottle off the floor and made sure its screw-top fit. The bottle had to be airtight. That's the first rule of flotation.

How many messages had he cast into the sea? So many he'd run out of paper. What could he say that he hadn't already said? How could anyone rescue him if he didn't know where he was? After rummaging in the cupboards he found a soggy paper bag and tried to write, but the paper disintegrated in his hand.

He took out his wallet and removed his last business card. It still looked impressive, still said NEAL NATHANSON, DIRECTOR OF SPECIAL COLLECTIONS, and had the name of the investment bank he worked for, the Wall Street address, phone number, and email. He turned the card over and thought about what to write, wondering how to sum up his situation as clearly and succinctly as possible.

He wrote the word *fucked* on the back of the card and slid it into the bottle.

Neal screwed on the top, giving it an extra twist to make sure it was tight, then staggered to the doorway.

He looked at the boat. It had been a pretty awesome boat, sleek and unadorned, as if designed by a Scandinavian architect. A Beneteau Oceanis 38.1. Neal knew that because he'd found the owner's manual. He wondered if it had any salvage value. Would his boss be able to recoup some of the money?

Neal figured that it would be the kind of boat he'd buy if he had an offshore account full of illegally skimmed millions and liked sailing, but he was now pretty sure he didn't like sailing.

He chucked the bottle out into the night and waited for the splash.

Neal might have dozed off, might have fallen into a mini-coma, if that's even a medical condition, but he woke with a start. He blinked, trying to get the abrasive crunch of salt out of his desiccated eyes. Was that a light? In the near distance? He blinked again, wondering if he was hallucinating.

But the light continued to glow, moving on a course perpendicular to wherever the current was taking him.

He needed to send a signal.

There was no power, no flare gun, no flashlight. Neal thought he could potentially ignite some tangles of rope, but they were hopelessly snagged in what was left of the rigging.

The dot of light was moving away. This required him to make an executive decision. He would explain it to his boss later.

Neal hobbled into the hold and lifted one of the large duffel bags stacked on the floor. He reached into a cubby and took a bottle of lighter fluid—something he'd considered drinking only a day ago. He carried them out to the front of the boat—the prow was what they called it—and unzipped the bag. He knew the duffels contained a mix of currency; there were euros and dollars, yen and yuan, and a grab bag of bills from various Caribbean islands and Mexico. Neal upended the bag, and neatly wrapped bricks of money fell onto the deck. He recognized some notes from the Dominican Republic—old-school guys on one side and a building that looked like a bad hotel on the other—and some Jamaican bills that had a pissed-off black man in a suit and tie on the front. The stack was almost three feet high; it was a lot of money, over a million US, but like the saying goes, "You can't take it with you if you're dead and the seagulls are pecking your eyes out."

Besides, it wasn't his money. Not exactly.

Neal emptied the lighter fluid on the bills and struck a match. The stack ignited with a *whoosh*, sending him tumbling backward. He scrambled away from the flames, crawling aft toward the cockpit.

He stood and scanned the horizon. The dot was still there, still visible. Maybe not a mirage after all.

The smell of burning resin and wood jolted him. The currency was burning, but now part of the boat was too. For a brief moment Neal considered getting a fire extinguisher and putting it out. But then what?

As the prow began to burn with real intent, Neal dragged the remaining duffel bags out of the hold and stacked them at the rear of the boat. They weren't that heavy, but there were nine of them. He stared at the bags. Why had he risked so much for money that wasn't even his? What had he been thinking? A burst of flames shot up. He remembered the life raft he'd discovered when he still had the energy to scavenge. He dragged it out and opened the lid, triggering automatic inflation. The life raft began to grow bigger and bigger, crowding the cockpit, forcing him to move and shuffle and try not to get knocked overboard by the very thing meant to save him. It took all his strength, but he managed to shove it over the side and into the water. He was careful to tie it so it didn't drift away and loaded the bags into it.

He looked toward the light. It appeared to be coming closer, but it was hard to see clearly now that the entire front half of the boat was engulfed in flames.

Chlöe zipped up her jacket and studied the guy she'd just hauled out of the life raft. He was, if she was being charitable, a fucking mess, ragged and smelly like kelp, like something that might wash up dead on a beach. She'd given him some water, warned him to drink slowly, and watched him guzzle it, puke all over himself, and then pass out on the deck. She didn't know if he was unconscious or dead—not that it made much difference to her; she'd have to put him ashore as soon as she could.

She had watched his boat sink. Funny how the ocean snuffed out the flames so abruptly—one minute it was a raging inferno, flames shooting fifteen feet into the air, plumes of black smoke swirling off the heat, and then it was gone, the stars returning and the water calm. Like flicking a switch.

She bent down. He looked completely stonkered, his face sun-roasted and peeling with a patchy, scruffy beard, and his arms and legs were pocked with scrapes and scabs and festering cuts. She could tell he wasn't a sailor; even in his emaciated state he was soft and doughy, like a corporate drone, a salaryman, maybe a dot-com billionaire trying to prove his manhood by going to sea. She could tell he was probably a nice-looking guy on a normal day. Cleaned up and drinking a bottle of Shiraz at a fancy restaurant, he might even be the kind of guy she found attractive. But then she liked men who were physically her equal, and they were hard to find.

Chlöe knew she should follow maritime protocol and relay news of the rescue to her team, but she didn't. Hers was supposed to be a solo circumnavigation, from Melbourne to Melbourne, a big spin around the globe without any companion. Would the media understand that she had saved this poor sucker's life, or would they call her a fraud for not being solo 100 percent of the time? She shuddered at the thought of what they'd say on social media. No one would hesitate to thoroughly shame her. The bad press would kill the project. Her sponsors would abandon it and then she'd be broke, ruined, an embarrassment for the rest of her life. A sane person would've let the guy go down with his ship.

She had prepared for all kinds of problems—de-mastings and shipwreck, shark attack and pirates—but rescuing someone was a complication she hadn't foreseen. She was hoping she could discreetly drop him off at the next small port, maybe Paramaribo in Suriname, and be back on her way without anybody noticing. For sure the guy couldn't complain; she'd saved his ass. And if he was some kind of big shot, maybe she'd get a new corporate sponsor. Every little bit helped.

Chlöe stepped over her unconscious passenger. It was close quarters; the cockpit of her boat was designed to be piloted by one person and wasn't what you'd call spacious. She squeezed past the duffels and into the galley. She'd caught a wahoo earlier that day, a twenty-five-pounder, and was keeping it cool in the sink. Normally a fish that size would feed her for a week, but her guest looked like he hadn't eaten in a while. He'd be hungry when he woke up.

She carried the fish out of the galley, slapped it down over the transom, and unclipped the folding knife from her shorts. She was about to gut the wahoo when she hesitated. She looked over at the guy, passed out on the deck. She noticed the rise and fall of his chest. In the excitement of rescuing him and watching his boat sink, she hadn't given a thought to what was in those duffel bags. She'd helped haul them aboard. What was so important that he saved them? Her satellite phone beeped. She picked it up and sent a quick SMS in reply. The midnight check-in was one of the protocols developed to keep her safe. She ducked into the cabin and scanned her instruments. Everything looked good. The GPS was still marking her location. There were no storms on the radar.

Chlöe squatted by one of the duffel bags, turned on her headlamp, and pulled the zipper. She wasn't sure what she would find. Drugs? Guns? A dozen severed heads? She was prepared for almost anything, but she actually gasped when she saw all that money. There was a lot of it. More than she would ever make in her life no matter how many corporate sponsors she had or how many times she sailed around the world.

She pulled out a neatly bundled stack of bills. They were mostly euros. Brick after brick of bright yellow two-hundred-euro notes. They were pretty: a picture of a doorway on one side, a bridge on the back. Chlöe laughed. A stack of these could open some doors, that's for sure. There were other bundles of euros: green hundreds, orange fifties, purplish five hundreds. She opened another bag and found that it was filled with American dollars. Bundles and bundles of crisp one-hundred-dollar bills. The dollar wasn't as pretty as the euro, but it gave off a kind of gravitas, a no-nonsense aura that took her breath away. Another bag held bills from India, with a picture of Gandhi, and Australian currency, green bills with a portrait of Dame Nellie Melba, the opera singer. Chlöe had to admit that it was strange to put an opera singer on money. Birds were more popular: pheasants on Taiwanese money, cranes on the Japanese yen, Canadian grosbeaks. But an opera singer was better than birds.

Chlöe hadn't grown up rich. Her parents owned a little seafood restaurant in Melbourne, a neighborhood place that had locally caught specials every day, although mostly they did a brisk business in takeaway fish and chips. It was her dad's love of fishing that meant she spent most of her childhood on the water. She learned to fish, she learned to sail, she learned to cook, which condemned her to a nomadic life of working on yachts, preparing gourmet dinners for the one-percenters, then trying to look the other way as the millionaires got drunk, popped Viagra, and mounted moisties half their age, screwing on the deck, acting as if the crew was invisible, just part of the furniture. The best trips were when she delivered the yachts: her and the crew sailing from Sydney to Macau or Bali, while the millionaires flew in their private jets.

She picked up a stack of Swiss francs. Where did this come from? What was the guy going to do with it? She knew what she'd do. If this was her money, she'd open her own restaurant in Melbourne, a classy wine bar that served fresh oysters. Then she'd buy one of those swank modern condos by the river. With this much cash she could be the one having a root on the deck of a yacht. She liked the sporty types—the pro golfers and surfers—sunburnt men who were gorgeous and blond and athletic, with big tools packed in their budgie smugglers. That was one of the things she learned working on millionaires' boats: the richer you are, the more attractive the lover you get.

With this much cash, she could do anything she wanted. For sure she wouldn't have to sail around the world trying to raise awareness for a fucking disease.

Neal opened his eyes and blinked up at the sky. The sun was breaking the horizon, the color changing from cool indigo to bright hot blue. He smacked his lips, feeling the flakes of dried skin and crackle of scabs.

"It's alive."

He turned toward the voice.

"I'll give you some water, but if you chunder on my deck again you can fucking swim home."

Neal tried to speak, his vocal cords making a salt-encrusted croak. He nodded and reached for the bottle but discovered his hand wouldn't move. His right hand had been lashed to the railing by some kind of industrial-strength plastic tie. Neal looked at the woman sitting behind him, a few feet away, her arms across the top of the steering wheel. She seemed to shrug, almost apologetic, and said, "Just a precaution."

He made another croaking sound.

She put the bottle in his left hand, which, oddly enough, wasn't tied to anything. He held the bottle to his lips and let a trickle drop onto his tongue. The water tasted sweet, like candy. A tremor ran through his arm and he was afraid he might spill it. He took another sip, then he glugged from the bottle and water leaked out of his cracked lips onto his face.

"Easy."

He nodded—he didn't want her to take the bottle away—and cleared his throat. "Thank you." He took another sip and said, "I thought I was going to die." Neal looked at her with what he hoped was an appropriately grateful and sincere expression. "My name is Neal. Neal Nathanson."

"You want something to eat? Neal?"

Neal tried to read her expression. She wasn't smiling. "If it's not too much trouble."

He watched as she walked through the companionway and stepped into the galley. He took another sip of water. The liquid slid down his throat and he could feel it bringing him back to life. He was going to be all right. He looked for the duffel bags. They were stacked on the deck, right where he left them. Except for the one he lit on fire, they were all here. Mission accomplished.

Losing the boat was the only downside. He'd have to explain that somehow. Maybe write it off as a travel expense. Otherwise, he'd done his job. He might even get a bonus this year. Maybe he could vacation in Paris. Eat a croissant. Meet a handsome Frenchman named Patrice.

He tugged at the plastic tie and it cut into his skin. He winced. What had he done to deserve that? He wasn't dangerous.

Then it occurred to him that maybe she was.

Neal felt a sharp pain in his ankle. Then another one. He opened his eyes and saw the woman holding a couple of plates. She was kicking him.

He didn't remember falling asleep. The sun was higher in the sky, blinding him.

"I caught a wahoo yesterday," she said.

He took the plate with his left hand and set it on his lap. A plastic spork was balanced on the edge. The smell of the pan-seared fish caused his stomach to knot and growl, and his saliva glands erupted, a thick strand of drool bursting out of his mouth. He looked at the fish, the rice and beans on the side, and briefly considered saying a prayer. Not that he was religious. He'd never believed in a higher power or karma or a sentient and benevolent universe. That was illogical, imaginary-friend thinking and he was a rational person, someone who believed in science. But all the same, he was feeling thankful, more thankful than he'd ever felt about anything in his life; he was happy to be alive.

Neal stifled a sob and said, "Wahoo."

She sat across from him in the cockpit, resting her arm on the tiller, and sporked some food into her mouth. Neal took a small bite of fish and chewed it. It was delicious. The best food he'd ever tasted. He balanced the plate on his knee and leaned toward it as far as his restraint would let him. If his hand hadn't been lashed to the railing, he would've buried his face in the food and wept for joy. Instead he reminded himself to go slow. Chew thoroughly. He didn't want to overwhelm his system.

He smiled. "This is so good. Seriously."

She didn't respond, just stared at him.

Neal took another bite, a bigger one, and looked around. It was a small boat, smaller than the one he'd lit on fire, and it had a big pink stripe down the middle and a matching one on the sail. The sail wasn't doing much, hanging there in the lack of breeze, and Neal saw a block of logos, the trademarks of corporations, festooned across it. He recognized the mermaid, the iconic apple with the bite taken out of it, the names of a Korean electronics manufacturer and a German car company.

"Are you in a race?"

She didn't respond. She just kept staring at him as she ate. Neal couldn't hold her gaze. She was too intense, or maybe he was too tired. Either way, he turned and looked out at the ocean. They were, it seemed, in the middle of nowhere. The sea totally calm.

"Where are we?"

She didn't reply. Neal shifted. He was starting to feel distinctly uncomfortable about his predicament. He could see that she was thinking about something. Sizing him up. Maybe she was considering all the different ways she could prepare and eat him.

Neal felt a shiver run up his spine. "Can you untie me?"

She finished her last bite and banged her plate against the hull, knocking the remaining rice into the ocean. She put the plate down and took a swig of water from a canteen. Then she looked him right in the eye:

"Tell me a story, Neal. Tell me about the money."

PREVIOUSLY, ONSHORE...

Bryan LeBlanc had never met a bigger bunch of assholes.

Sure, they were smart and hardworking. Strivers, you'd call them—the kind of people who worked eighty hours a week and never complained. They'd sit at their desks for days staring at multiple monitors—images flickering and flashing and scrolling—lined up in the open-plan office like dairy cows at milking stations, hooked to machines that sucked the life out of them. And they loved it.

They had no social life to speak of. No friends outside the business. They were surfing the algorithm, riding the markets in new and ever more complex machinations, shooting the tube to wrest lucre from the system and deposit it in the treasury of their employer. They would pull all-nighters, forget to sleep. Crank the outcomes. Crunch the numbers. And after the numbers had been crunched and victory tasted, they'd shower in the gym. Whatever it took to make their nut, to get their bonus, to taste some of that sweet honey. They saw themselves as the heroes of the free market, the US Marines of capitalism. They were the few, the proud, the completely full of themselves. This was the corporate culture encouraged by the big shots at InterFund.

Why would they dedicate themselves so ferociously to their jobs?

A sane person might wonder.

Bryan considered himself a sane person. But he knew why they did it.

The answer—and this came as no surprise to anyone—was to be rich. And not just rich enough to have a nice house and go on cool vacations and eat at trendy restaurants. The goal was to be superrich, the kind of wealthy where you got to bully and humiliate your fellow human beings. The kind of rich where you had butlers and drivers and cooks and a private jet, where you could drink champagne and get your cock sucked by your trophy wife on your way to play a round of golf with the president of the United States of America. That's what these assholes were after. They wanted privilege and access—the access to more money and the privilege to take it for themselves. That's why they sat in front of their computer monitors, bleary-eyed and amped up on a cocktail of Adderall or Ritalin and whatever was the benzodiazepine du jour. That's why they left it all on the field and gave 200 percent and strove to dominate from above. It baffled Bryan that they would say these things, like they meant anything, as if they were actual measurements of competence and not just mantras of the deluded. But they did say these things. They bundled and bought and swapped and sold and shorted and traded.

And then they high-fived each other.

Bryan looked at the monitor on his left. He had seven screens on his desk streaming business news and market reports from around the world, with several dedicated to his foreign exchange trading, and one where he could check his emails and follow political news streaming through various feeds he subscribed to.

When he tried to explain what he did to other people in the company, or even his clients, he could see their eyes glaze over in less than sixty seconds. Foreign exchange trading was a complex transaction and required attention to minutiae: the weather reports, political maneuverings, and the random comings and goings of people in far-flung places like Bangladesh and Botswana, Berlin and Buenos Aires—the kinds of things that most people couldn't be bothered with. Bryan had spent his youth in his bedroom playing video games on his Xbox and PS2, and this wasn't much different; all you needed was the ability to stay single-mindedly focused on the screen for hours and to have fast fingers when it was time to pounce.

Most brokers liked simple deals: IPOs and stock surges. The shorthand of buy, hold, sell. People didn't want to look at the tiny details that made up the big picture. That was like doing math, and math was hard. So if you were someone who was adept at this, someone with an eye for the connectivity of small details to the wider world, you had an edge, you could find an opportunity and exploit the fuck out of it.

Which was how the whole global financial meltdown happened in the first place.

"I don't know if you know this, but there's something called sunlight where you're going. You'll need this."

Bryan looked up from his screen as Seo-yun Kim, his boss and the managing director of the foreign exchange division, handed him a bottle of sunscreen.

Bryan read the label. "I didn't know they made an SPF 110."

"It shows I care."

Bryan smiled. "I like your scarf."

She tugged at the bright red scarf wrapped around her neck. "My fiancé gave it to me. He said it makes him happy when I wear it."

It was a departure from her typical uniform of a black suit and white blouse. Seo-yun took the scarf off and held it out at arm's length, as if it were contaminated. Bryan laughed. "I'm guessing it doesn't make you happy."

She dropped it onto his desk. "My happiness isn't the reason he gave me a scarf." She flipped her fingers through her hair. "Can I get you to leave your desk for some sushi?"

Bryan nodded. "Let's go."

They sat at the counter and, not for the first time, Bryan wondered why sushi restaurants were always austere. The food was simple, with almost no embellishment, just rice and fish with a skid mark of wasabi. So why did the restaurant match the food? What was that about?

He watched as Seo-yun expertly used her chopsticks to place a slice of pickled ginger in her mouth without smudging her lipstick. She turned to him. "I'm here for the ginger. I don't really care about the fish."

A waitress brought a cold beer and poured it into a glass.

"Sorry. Beginning my vacation early," Bryan said.

"I'm jealous."

"You'll get your honeymoon soon enough."

That brought a groan from Seo-yun. "This wedding is going to kill me."

Bryan raised an eyebrow. He hoped Seo-yun would continue talking. Although they'd worked together for almost four years, he didn't know much about her. She was considered something of an anomaly in the company, an eccentric and a loner who people said was "on the spectrum." She had risen to a position of power in the firm because she was amazing at her job; she had an almost intuitive grasp of what was happening in the world and could make connections that he couldn't even see. And he was good, excellent even, at reading the data and making calls. Seo-yun was in a different league. Some colleagues hated working with her and tried to undermine her. But Bryan admired Seo-yun's talent and liked her management style. She was direct. She didn't play games. She had a complete lack of charm that he found charming. They weren't close friends, but they got along well and had an easy professional relationship. Out of the office she kept to herself. Her personal life was a mystery. He didn't even know her fiancé's name.

The sushi chef placed a blue crab hand roll in front of each of them. Seo-yun hesitated, as if she might say more about her impending nuptials, but instead she stuffed half the hand roll into her mouth and bit down hard.

Bryan didn't say anything. He watched as she chewed.

Seo-yun reached over and picked up his beer. She took a long sip. "Sorry. Wasabi."

"Happy to share."

She suppressed a burp and said, "I don't know what's happening to me, but ever since I agreed to get married I haven't felt the same."

"That's normal, I think."

"Really?"

Bryan nodded. "Isn't that why people do it? So they don't feel the same after?"

Seo-yun finished his beer. "Control is a funny thing. Who's in control. How you control yourself. So many decisions." She sighed. "It's hard to find any pleasure in it."

*   *   *

On their walk back from the sushi restaurant, Bryan told Seo-yun that while he was gone his holdings were all automated: if currencies fluctuated outside certain ranges, trades would be triggered automatically. Barring a financial catastrophe like the near default in Greece or some sort of war breaking out, everything should be on cruise control. She told him she'd cover if there was a problem, and that while she didn't enjoy vacationing herself, she wanted him to have a good time. He'd obviously been stressed out the last few months.

"Stress kills," she said.

It was true. He'd been on a roll, pulling in millions for the company and making his name as a producer, a rainmaker, an AT-fucking-M. In the corporate hierarchy, Seo-yun was his boss, but she was smart enough to let him do his own thing. She never looked over his shoulder or ran an audit. That was what made her a great manager. It was also her weakness.

Back at his desk, Bryan watched the euro oscillate. There was no reason for it to behave that way, nothing that he could see. But money was weird. Sometimes it did what it wanted and you had to be willing to go along for the ride.

He looked at his phone and saw that it was five o'clock. He put his computer to sleep and slipped into his suit jacket. He pulled his tie tight around his neck. The dress code was another thing he hated about his job. Why wear an expensive suit to look at a computer all day? He could do the job in his underwear. Honestly, he'd prefer to do the job in his underwear. The suit was just another piece of the bullshit they were selling. The power suit. Dress for success. Fuck you.

He closed his office door, listening for the click of the latch locking behind him, and gave his assistant a nod. Then he walked past the bullpen—a place that sometimes gave off the waft of body odor and ass—without looking at the young traders hustling their next buck, busting their butts for bottles of single malt Scotch and weekends in Vegas. Bryan knew they hated him for leaving at five. But they knew he was in before them, dealing with currency trades from Europe, so they couldn't be too snarky. Besides, it's not like he cared what they thought; he wasn't coming back.

Seo-yun Kim was not stupid. She knew that she was difficult or awkward or special—whatever word they wanted to use to say that she wasn't interested in the usual bullshit. She was good at logic and numbers. She liked systems. What she didn't like were people who got emotional. Too much emotion was detrimental. Emotional people made bad decisions. Naturally, she recognized emotion when she saw it or heard it or read about it. At work she was clinical and analytical—you can't deal with vast volumes of capital if you get caught up in feelings. That's when you start making mistakes. But most people did get emotional and she was adept at reading how these feelings might affect the value of a particular currency. Brexit was a good example. The pound might have lost 17 percent of its value overnight, but she saw it coming and made some serious bank for the firm. She was not stupid.

She also had an uncanny ability to compartmentalize her life. At work she was organized, rigorous, and serious. She didn't hang around the break room gossiping or dropping humblebrags like the other employees. That didn't mean she wouldn't socialize from time to time. There were people whom she was friendly with—maybe not friends, but they would have lunch together occasionally. And as much as she hated the expression *happy hour*, she would sometimes join her colleagues for an after-work cocktail. She liked to keep her personal life separate from her business life. Did that make her a bad person?

It was an easy walk from her office to the Rector Street subway station. From there she would jump onto a train, hop off at Prince Street, and in a few minutes be at her condo in West SoHo, located in a parcel of Manhattan carved out by real estate speculators trying to create a market for wealthy young strivers. It worked. Seo-yun loved her building, a converted factory with large windows and exposed brick—it was high-end living with an artsy edge. When she first visited the model apartment, she had tried to buy it just the way it was. The real estate agent gave her the number of the interior designer and Seo-yun had her apartment designed to look like a replica of the model. It wasn't cozy; it was modern and clean. Her parents visited and said it "lacked Seoul." They sent her a traditional Korean ink brush painting of mountains and blossoming trees along a tranquil river that now dominated her living room.

She didn't understand her friends' and parents' insistence that she needed to make it more her own. Why did it need to reflect her personality? She lived with her personality 24/7; she didn't need to come home to it after work.

For a few years she had brunch every Sunday with some of her classmates from graduate school. They were all successful women, but as a few got married or moved away, their numbers had dwindled. Now it was Seo-yun and Stacy and Annie, a lesbian couple who'd been together since college. The conversations had become domestic. They used to talk about politics and sex and music, but now she found herself getting drawn into their personal disputes, as if she were a licensed therapist, as if she cared where they bought their summer home. She wondered if she would still go to brunch after she was married.

Why was she getting married?

She was attractive in a kind of intimidating way, so she never had a problem getting men interested in her. It was her personality that they found problematic, her tendency to be bluntly honest, when all they wanted to hear was a soft lie. If you don't want to hear the truth, don't ask: "Was it good for you?" Her parents were afraid she wouldn't find anyone who would overlook her special personality, and it wasn't like the thought hadn't occurred to her too. So when her boyfriend asked her to marry him, she thought, *Why not? What's the worst that could happen?*

Her smartphone chirped on the breakfast bar: a text from her fiancé. He was offering to pick up sandwiches from Café Habana so they could sit down and look at the websites of various wedding photographers. He'd found one who had gone to Cooper Union and was really pushing the envelope of what wedding photography was all about.

Seo-yun sighed. When had her fiancé become relentless? She typed, "I don't care," but then deleted it. Instead, she told him to bring beer.

Bryan stopped by his apartment near Battery Park just long enough to pick up his mail, nod at the doorman, and change out of his suit. It was a nice enough place: generic and luxurious, the kind of address where a successful Wall Street mover and shaker should live. The rent was exorbitant. Some people might be impressed, but not him. Bryan looked out the window at the view, at the river and the lights of New Jersey twinkling in the distance. What kind of person pays a small fortune for a view of New Jersey? An asshole, that's who.

Dressed in blue jeans and a white shirt under a simple jacket, he left the pin-striped suit and polished brogues in the closet, his briefcase on the breakfast bar, and took the subway across the river to his father's apartment. It was a funky one-bedroom in a tenement building in Long Island City, but since his father's death last year he'd kept paying the rent, preferring the mix of artists and what was left of the old-school working-class vibe to the phony luxe of Battery Park City. He thought of his father's place as his safe house, somewhere he could go to unwind, a home that made him feel normal.

He stopped for dinner at a pizzeria on Vernon Boulevard. While he sat there he got a text from a woman he'd been dating. It wasn't a serious relationship, although he could tell that she thought he should be proposing any day now. She was, after all, the kind of well-educated, good-looking woman that Wall Street wizards were supposed to marry.

A cute emoji popped up on his phone: a tiny cartoon of a Chinese take-out box and chopsticks, followed by two champagne bottles and what looked like a flamenco dancer. He knew she was disappointed that he was going off on vacation by himself and guessed she was offering to pick up some takeout and come over to his place for drinks and horizontal dancing, a kind of desperate last grab for an all-expense-paid Caribbean getaway. But that wasn't going to happen. He didn't bother to reply. Nothing personal. It was his signal to her that he'd already gone to sleep. It helped that he got to work before sunrise. His job was a good excuse for a lot of things.

She was attracted to him because he was successful. He made a lot of money, and that made him a good catch. Even if he'd behaved like one of his porcine colleagues, she probably would've liked him. Boys will be boys, and rich boys will be the most boyish of all. Sometimes, when he was on top of her, thrusting away, he'd look down and see her face going through the motions, as if her world were getting rocked, instead of her just putting in her time on the way to making some bank. It made him sick. Not so repulsed that he couldn't ejaculate. She wasn't a monster.

Bryan sipped his wine. If his father were still alive he would have made fun of him for ordering the most obscure glass on the menu. *What's the difference between that and Two Buck Chuck?* Of course any attempt to explain organic viniculture or the influence of terroir would be mocked. Making Bryan feel like a pretentious blowhard was one of his father's favorite games. Which was weird because his father was a wannabe poet, and expounding on the foibles of other writers was all he ever did.

He'd been a high school English teacher, but after Bryan's mother died his father retired to the small apartment, where he spent his days writing poems and thinking of himself as some kind of Queens flaneur. Bryan laughed; if his father thought he was pretentious for ordering a nice wine, he should've heard himself pontificating about Robert Lowell and W. S. Merwin, or the work of Louise Glück; about how the new poets were bullshit and how the Beats were overrated phonies.

It took six months to clean the apartment out. There was so much stuff to go through. Stacks of books. Why did his father buy poetry collections in foreign languages? Was he really reading Cavafy in Greek? Apollinaire in French? Mayakovski in Russian? He didn't speak any language but English. Bryan donated his father's books to the local library; he hoped it could make some use of them.

As for the ratty collection of composition notebooks, Bryan didn't really know what to do. There were hundreds of them. He'd flipped through a few, read some of his father's poems, his musings, his rants. His father wasn't famous—he'd published maybe ten poems in his entire life—so Bryan couldn't donate the archives to a university. He asked a couple of his dad's old friends if they wanted to sort through the notebooks, but they didn't have time, weren't interested, or were engaged in some kind of Japanese-influenced declutter program and didn't want anything that didn't spark joy. In the end, Bryan carted them down to the curb and dumped them in the recycling bins.

With his father's things cleared out and some new paint on the walls, the place looked cozy and clean. Bryan decided to stay there on the weekends. It was small and had an unreliable furnace, but it was normal. It was, as his father would say, authentic. A real apartment in the kind of real life that real people should lead. Grounded. Humble. In a part of the city where people actually made things or fixed things, worked with their hands. It was the opposite of the airy-fairy financial fantasyland that Bryan was a part of.

He didn't know why—maybe it was the constant stream of derision his father subjected him to about Wall Street corruption and fat cats destroying the world—but he never felt comfortable surrounded by the trappings of wealth. There wasn't anything wrong with being rich. Not really. But there was something his father said that rang true: "Rich people just aren't very nice."

The managing directors of all the departments were meeting in a large glass conference room with a large glass conference table. As the directors entered, they passed a white marble counter lined with trays of pastries, fresh fruit in cups, carafes of orange juice, and a large thermos filled with hot coffee. No one touched the food. Ever. Seo-yun didn't know why. Why couldn't she eat a pain au chocolat while other people were talking? But no one ever did. Perhaps it was some kind of macho thing—a display of willpower and restraint to make up for the extravagance of their lives. Somehow not eating a muffin in the morning translated into buying a Maserati in the afternoon. There was no time for pleasure when there was money to be made.

She wasn't the only woman in the room, but she was the only Asian American working at this level in the company. Even though the room was crowded, with several managing directors joining via Skype from overseas, there wasn't even an African American diversity hire present. Everyone else was white.

The managing director of bond trading was getting into an argument with the director of analytics. The director of analytics was unpopular at the firm because he never stopped reminding people he went to Harvard and he always brought statistics to shoot down the complex—and often crackpot—schemes that were floated in these meetings. Seo-yun appreciated his logic. She didn't care where he went to school.

A couple of MDs were droning on about volatility in various sectors of the economy. Real estate continued to perform, but pharmaceuticals and biotech were looking shaky. The gas and oil lobby in Washington, DC, had gotten some new law passed and extraction was hot again.

These discussions didn't interest her; they didn't intersect with her job, so she was rarely asked to be part of the conversation. In fact, she couldn't remember the last time she spoke at one of these weekly meetings, not that she wanted to speak. As long as her department was bringing in massive profits, she could let her work do the talking.

Seo-yun looked down at her tablet and saw that the ruble was making a move. That was unusual. She sent a message to the other forex traders on her team.

"How do you think that will affect the riyal? Miss Kim?"

Seo-yun looked up. A dozen business suits were staring at her. She had no idea which one of them had asked the question.

"The riyal?" She smiled. "It's the ruble we should be watching. It's starting to move."

The executive director nodded and said, "What does LeBlanc think? I'm thinking this news will destabilize the Saudis. Can you get him to shoot me an email about the riyal?"

Seo-yun felt her stomach drop. "Bryan's on vacation, but I'll put together some analysis for you today."

"Great. Send it to the group."

The meeting ended. Seo-yun grabbed a pain au chocolat on her way out the door and jammed it into her jacket pocket. She went into the women's restroom, into the nearest stall, and closed the lid. She pulled the pain au chocolat from her pocket, sat down, and began to eat. She let the crumbs scatter on her black jacket and felt the chocolate melt in her mouth, coating her tongue with a rich and sweet and slightly bitter flavor.

Bryan turned the Sunfish into the breeze, letting the sail flutter for a moment before it picked up the wind again and carried the boat forward. He'd gotten pretty good at sailing. For almost a year he'd spent his Sunday afternoons taking lessons at the Manhattan Sailing School, going out and cruising the Hudson in a J/24, taking turns at the helm, and hoisting sails with a small group of enthusiasts. The best part was that they talked about boats and sails and knots, about wind and waves, about the nuances of reading the weather. He didn't know what anyone else in his class did; the others didn't know he worked on Wall Street. There was no social climbing, no one-upmanship—it was about being on the water.

He kept the Sunfish beyond the breaking waves but close to shore. It made no sense to go out into the open ocean in a small boat. Besides, he didn't have anything to prove, and he was having an excellent time zipping back and forth across the little bay. It was a beautiful day, the water off Punta Cana was clear, and there was a steady wind.

He looked back at the line of palm trees that marked the resort; under them a hundred chaise lounges were set out in rows across the sand, facing the ocean as if it was going to teach them something. No wonder this part of the Dominican Republic was called the Coconut Coast. You could plop your ass in a chair and have people bring you food and drink all day long. It was the perfect break from the maniacal pace of Wall Street, a chance to check out and recharge.

That was the dream, wasn't it? Drop out of the rat race and spend your days barefoot, slightly drunk, and sunburnt in a tropical paradise. His father had always said he wanted to retire to Hawaii, but when Bryan offered to take him there on vacation he declined. He didn't even want to go to Florida, and the Keys were supposed to be a poet's paradise.

No stress. No meetings. He didn't have to watch every twitch and tick of the dollar against the yuan. The S&P 500 could go fuck itself. There was no ass-kissing, no marketing directives, no bullshit. Yet when he walked past the sunbathers on the beach, almost all of them were looking at their tablets or their smartphones, checking whatever it was they were checking, complaining about the Wi-Fi, bitching about the broadband speed.

Bryan turned the boat, ducking the boom as he came about. A psychiatrist might've had a theory about why he was there: he was making amends by living the authentic life his father always wanted but never could have—something like that. But then psychiatry wasn't really a science, so maybe it was all a bunch of bull. His dad would have agreed with that for sure.

Seo-yun glanced at her fiancé. "Sorry."

He sighed and put down his fork. "Soy. C'mon. All you do is work. We've got a wedding to plan."

Seo-yun didn't respond. What could she say? Was there anything more boring than planning a wedding? But it seemed that all he wanted to do was go over his ideas. He was consumed by details: the food, the flowers, the music, the invitations. He even tried to show her samples of fabric for the tablecloths. Who did that? Who cared about that stuff? She spent her days looking at financial minutiae; the last thing she wanted to do on her lunch hour was obsess about other kinds of details. Couldn't the tablecloth be white? Couldn't they hire a wedding planner like normal people? As long as everyone had a good time—and with what this wedding was going to cost they'd better have a good time—did it really matter if the napkins matched the flower arrangements? Did he have to call them serviettes?

"Soy? Please."

She held up a finger, silencing him, and read the text from her assistant. There was a routine inquiry from compliance about a drawdown on a margin account. It was an unrecognized transaction and the client was concerned. She typed in a quick reply. "It's important."

He nodded, letting his floppy bangs droop over his sweaty pink forehead. When they'd first started dating she liked his style, how he looked like the edgy singer in an emo band; but now he just looked like an overweight marketing exec who was trying too hard to look like the edgy singer in an emo band.

He reached across the table and tapped on her wrist. "Am I really supposed to give your parents a goose? I don't even know where to find one."

"You can give them a wooden goose or a picture of a goose. It's symbolic."

"Seems a little silly."

"Just be happy you don't have to wear a *jeogori*."

Seo-yun signaled the waiter for the check. She heard a disgruntled snort blare from her fiancé's nostrils, the sound he made when he was unhappy. She watched him tug on his mustache, another sign he was annoyed.

She shrugged. "I have to go."

His lips turned into a smug kind of pout. "I thought your bank was too big to fail."

She wanted to tell him that whatever was happening at work was way more interesting than fretting over the design of the invitation or about the availability of pink peonies for the arrangements. She wanted to tell him that this whole marriage thing was a mistake, that his control-freak micromanaging of the wedding plans had killed any affection she felt for him, that she couldn't stand the sound of his voice or the sight of his pouty mouth, that she would never be able to enjoy sex with him again, that she didn't even want to be friends. Instead she said, "If the bank fails, we'll have to get married at city hall."

She heard him snort again as she left the restaurant. Once she was out on the street, she imagined herself never seeing him again and, for the first time in days, felt a lightness in her step.

Seo-yun's office was really a bunker for the thirteen computer monitors arrayed around her like some kind of monetary mission control, with piles of documents and folders acting as a backdrop. She closed the door, put her smartphone on her desk as she kicked off her shoes. She sat down and rolled her chair into position. As she waited for the account to load she realized that everything in her life had suddenly become annoying: her job, her fiancé, the wedding, the fact that she had to cover for her colleague, her lack of any time for herself. It was all a bit much. Bryan should be here to deal with this; it wasn't her normal thing; she didn't manage institutional accounts. LeBlanc was something of a savant when it came to currency trading, and Seo-yun wasn't egomaniacal enough to deny that he'd been partly responsible for the stellar performance of her division. Not that he did it by himself; she'd made some major moves too. She liked to think that it wasn't about individual effort; it was the team that won the game.

It didn't take long for her to see that almost half a million dollars had been taken on margin against the account. What happened to it was unclear. It had initially been converted to Swiss francs, but after that, it seemed to go to an account at a Russian bank. The Russian account was closed, the funds vanishing in a maze of transactions. This, she realized, was a knot that was going to take some time to untangle. It bothered her that the client hadn't been paying attention. That was the problem with these institutions and endowments: they didn't check the details of their finances, and then when something went wrong, they freaked out and blamed everyone else. They just assumed that their wealth bubbled from a magical fountain somewhere. Seo-yun realized she was being unfair. These clients had hired her company to safeguard their pension funds and college endowments.

She saw LeBlanc's assistant walking past. Why couldn't she remember his name? Was it Chad? Brad? Chip? She opened her door and waved him over.

"Hey. Do you have a number where I can reach Bryan?"

The assistant, whom Seo-yun thought of as a surprisingly uptight young man from California, blinked at her. "I can try his cell."

Seo-yun nodded—she'd heard that supervisors and managers should nod; it showed empathy.

"Tell him to call me, okay?"

"I'll shoot him a text."

"While you're waiting to hear from him, can you work with compliance and trace some transactions for me?"

The assistant shifted from foot to foot. She could tell he wasn't comfortable with her question. "It's probably a glitch."

LeBlanc's assistant came up empty. Not only was he unable to follow the string of transactions on the missing money, but he couldn't get Bryan on the phone.

It was unusual. If something strange was going on here, what was happening in his other accounts? She used her password override and opened his files. Now that she knew what she was looking for, it didn't take long to find another account with a mysterious half million dollars drawn on its margin and used to execute a string of forex trades until the money vanished. She checked another account. This one had more headroom and was hit for a million dollars. Same thing. She opened another. Again, the margin loan, the maze of forex transactions.

She wondered whom to call. She didn't want to sound an alarm. Maybe this was how LeBlanc made money for his clients. Borrowing on margin wasn't a crime; in fact it was pretty common. There was probably a legitimate explanation for this.

Her phone rang. It was her fiancé. They were scheduled to go to a tasting with the wedding sommelier. She told him it would have to wait. Or he'd have to go spit in a bucket by himself.

Bryan finished writing a postcard to his ex-girlfriend. He didn't expect her to understand the message, but it also didn't matter—she was already pissed that he hadn't taken her on the trip. The idea was that she'd give the card to whomever the bank hired to track him down. He handed the postcard to the concierge and then strolled through the lobby. The architecture at the resort was open and breezy; it seemed that everything, the roof included, was made of rattan. He wondered if rattan was native to the Dominican Republic or if it was imported, like the chaise lounges and beach umbrellas—accessories for the globalization of leisure.

Outside he was hit by a gust of fetid air. This wasn't Martha's Vineyard or the Hamptons, this was off the grid in the DR, and down here the air was dense with a salt-scented funk, laced with the distinct aroma of sewage. That was the thing about humanity. People shit. Every day. Everywhere. You could treat it with chemicals or bury it in the ground or dump it into the ocean, but just like money, the stench followed you. Which sounded exactly like something his father would say.

Bryan nodded to several of the couples he'd chatted with the last few days. He hadn't been antisocial; he was out having fun, making acquaintances, generously overtipping the staff. People would remember him and that's what he wanted.

A couple of middle-aged women on a girlfriend getaway waved to him as they went up to the buffet. He smiled back. He'd flirted with them a bit. No harm in that. But he wasn't going to flirt with them this morning. He was starting to feel anxious.

He wasn't a big fan of the buffet. The food was exactly what you would find at a hotel in Orlando or on a cruise ship. Bryan picked up a plate and piled it with fresh fruit. He'd overdone it with the regional cuisine at the Caribbean celebration last night, eating a double helping of mofongo, a garlicky plantain mash that subsequently acted like Spackle in his gut. If he really was planning to spend the rest of his life traveling the world, seeing new places and eating like the locals, he'd have to get used to exotic foods. Or maybe it was the stress of what he'd done that was causing his gastrointestinal distress.

He had no idea what they knew. It was tempting to log in to the InterFund server and check his email to see what, if anything, was happening, but that was dangerous. They could trace the IP address of the hotel. It was the same reason he'd left his cell phone in the apartment in Long Island City—he didn't want them to track him down with that. He'd buy one of those prepaid phones when he got where he was going.

The hope was the managing directors wouldn't figure out what he'd done until they realized he hadn't returned from his vacation. They'd suspect something, maybe an accident that left him unconscious in a hospital somewhere, or maybe that he'd cracked and gone AWOL. It had happened before. One bond trader had gone to visit his mother for her birthday and six months later turned up living on the streets of Varanasi.

Bryan knew that eventually they would get around to unlocking his computer and going through his accounts. It would take them a couple of days, more or less, and then they'd know he'd ripped them off. If his plan succeeded, he'd leave this resort and have a few days to create a false trail. Then he could collect his money and disappear. Bryan thought he'd been smart about it, thought he'd covered his tracks, but he worried that he might have made a mistake, might have underestimated Seo-yun or whatever tech person they were sure to put on his case. Maybe they'd figure it out sooner. For all he knew, they could be on their way to the Dominican Republic right now. He reflexively looked over his shoulder and then, seeing sunbathers rubbing lotion on their bodies, heaved a sigh.

Who knew being a criminal was so stressful?

He'd justified ripping off the company a hundred times in his mind. They never hesitated to exploit the weaknesses of others, so why shouldn't others exploit them right back? Just the thought of the little guys, John Q. Public and Jane Doe, investing their life savings in a rigged game—a system that sanctioned corruption and insider trading, a money-churning behemoth that spit out trades every nanosecond for the banks—the unfairness of it all nagged at him like a fleabite that wouldn't go away. But then everyone knew that was the way Wall Street worked. People had seen the movies and the television shows; they'd read the newspapers or watched the human megaphone of Occupy denounce the corruption of the financial markets. Everyone knew it was a fucking scam, but nobody did anything: not the regulatory commission, not the Justice Department, certainly not the president or anyone who wanted to remain in politics for more than a week. But he did something. Bryan LeBlanc acted. He abused the trust of his clients, the trust of his employer, and he ripped the motherfuckers off. No matter what happened, that was the one thing he could be proud of.

His colleagues would probably make fun of him for stealing so little. Why not aim high? Shoot for the moon? He hadn't pulled off anything as lucrative and terrible as the subprime mortgage scam. That was a case of institutional greed, corporate perfidy where one group of people who weren't so great at math exploited the mortgage industry and made and then lost a fortune. That was because the people who were good at math saw the weakness in the scheme and shorted the subprime market. They became instant billionaires. In the parlance of his colleagues, they killed it. Too bad the rest of the world was collateral damage.

Bryan's scam was smaller, quieter, and only affected Inter-Fund. It was, he thought, an elegant kind of larceny.

Bryan would issue fake drawdown notices from his clients, stating they wanted the funds moved to a new account. Bryan had set up bank accounts in Moscow, Copenhagen, Singapore, and Dubai. He would switch things up to avoid suspicion, opening accounts in various banks under his clients' names, but all the accounts were actually controlled by a Portuguese lawyer Bryan paid a fat commission to. From there Bryan would play a shell game with the money involving a complex sequence of currency transactions that bounced it from account to account, country to country, currency to currency, until it discreetly slid into a shell account in the Caymans. It worked because his clients were all institutions and endowments and wouldn't notice the transactions unless they did an audit.

On a typical morning he'd borrow a few hundred thousand against one of his clients' accounts and send it to Moscow. From the Moscow account he'd buy Indian rupees. After he had a cup of coffee, he'd swap the rupees for Singapore dollars—INR/SGD—that he would hold for a few hours. Then, if the Singapore dollars moved a pip or two against another currency, he'd swap them again, buying some Kuwaiti dinars—SGD/KWD. These he would flip into rubles—KWD/RUB—do a quick RUB/DKK, then deposit the money in a numbered account in Copenhagen. After lunch he'd take out that money, convert it to Thai baht—DKK/THB—and then dump the money into Hong Kong dollars, which would sit overnight in an account in Macau. In the morning he'd buy Panamanian balboas—HKD/PAB—and that money would be sent to a private Panamanian bank before being transferred into the account of a corporate shell company in the Caymans. From there he would have his proxy—a junior bank manager in George Town—snatch up as much hard currency as he could and deposit it in a safe-deposit box.

Bryan wasn't greedy; greed made people stupid. He knew that eventually the market would suffer a correction and the loans would get called, or that one or more of his clients would read the fine print on their monthly statement and wonder what the hell was going on. There was only a small window, a few months, to pull the embezzlement off. In the end he'd banked $17 million, more than enough to let him disappear permanently.

Once he was out of the USA, his chances of avoiding prosecution were pretty good. He didn't think the company would bring in the police or FBI; it couldn't afford the bad PR that would come from a broker stealing from clients. And the clients wouldn't take the hit; the company would refund all their money. No one would want to make a big stink, the firm would absorb the loss, and the status quo would remain status quo. Any admission of a problem, any sudden revelation of fact—it was too scary for people.

Now that he was out of the country, he was basically free. Although there was always the chance that everything could go south in a moment.

At the same time, he was starting to regret his decision. Why hadn't he just resigned? Did he really want to live the rest of his life looking over his shoulder? Maybe he should've moved to some city like Nashville and opened a gourmet shop. Do it the honest way. They probably needed a gourmet store in Nashville. He'd import anchovies and olive oil from Spain, make his own burrata. That could be a nice life.

Did all criminals have remorse?

Bryan guessed that the sociopathic ones did not. But he did. Which maybe meant that he wasn't a sociopath. That was good news. While he was plotting the crime, he'd looked up the definition in one of his father's dictionaries. A sociopath was someone who was antisocial, with impaired empathy and impaired remorse, coupled with bold, rash, uninhibited behavior. Bryan didn't think of himself as antisocial; he just didn't like the douchebags he worked with. Otherwise he had a few friends. He socialized with the people at the sailing club. He went on dates. And while it was hard to empathize with faceless corporate profiteers, he was feeling remorse. That was proof right there.

An onshore wind picked up and Bryan had to hold his straw hat on his head as he walked to the beach. He settled into a chaise lounge underneath a small thatched roof and signaled the waitress. Everyone seemed to be drinking cocktails with wedges of pineapple cantilevered off the glass, but he asked for a beer. A Presidente.

One more day of vacation, and then it was time to disappear.

Neal Nathanson sat in the Starbucks not far from his office and read the email on his phone. It appeared that one of the senior vice presidents had gone missing and, perhaps worse, might have misappropriated funds. Not a small amount of money either. The director of compliance wanted him to check out the broker's apartment and see if he was there. Right. Like you'd misplace a few million dollars and then sit around your condo in your underwear watching reality TV on your new big screen. Still, it was his job to look into these kinds of things. He was good at finding people and even better at getting money back.

Neal looked up when a lean and handsome lumberjack walked over. It took him a second, but Neal recognized the lumberjack as his ex-boyfriend Bart.

"You're wearing flannel now?"

Bart grimaced and shook his head. "C'mon, man, don't be that way."

Neal let his head drop. "Sorry. I'm just . . . You've been working out."

"Rock climbing. You should try it."

They were careful not to lock eyes, and then Neal said, "It's pretty quiet around the house without you." He tried not to look completely miserable when he said it.

Bart stroked his beard. "It's only been a couple of months. It gets better."

This was a private joke between them and Neal couldn't help it, he let out a chuckle. He looked up and Bart was smiling. Neal smiled. "You okay out in Brooklyn?"

Bart nodded. "Red Hook is cool."

Bart pulled a key from his jeans pocket and put it on the table in front of Neal.

"Time you got this."

Neal took the key and held it. "I'll keep forwarding your mail and stuff."

"Thanks."

They stared at each other for a moment, and then Neal said, "I've got to get to work."

Bart patted him on the shoulder. "You're a workaholic."

"You always said that."

"Because it's true."

Bart turned to walk out of the Starbucks. Neal couldn't help noticing how he was rocking his tight jeans and an amazing pair of hand-tooled work boots.

"Nice boots."

"Thanks. A guy I know in Brooklyn made them."

Neal hated these apartment buildings. They were built in a corporate style that made them look intentionally architectural yet bland. The buildings stood shoulder to shoulder across Battery Park City, like a massive fence built to keep the breeze from getting to lower Manhattan. If Godzilla ever did clamber out of the Hudson, Neal hoped these would be the first to get stomped. He entered the lobby and checked in with the security guard at the front desk.

The guard called the management agent, who called the building manager, who told the super to deal with it. The super came out of a door behind the front desk and nodded at Neal.

"You don't look like a Wall Street guy."

Neal nodded and followed the super to the elevators. Why didn't he look like a Wall Street guy? He worked on Wall Street. But then he wasn't one of those clean-shaven, gray-suit-and-striped-tie guys. He preferred suede shoes to the crisp glint of polished leather, and his facial hair was scruffy. But he wasn't a slob; he was wearing a sport coat and crisp charcoal-colored jeans.

He looked at the building manager and said, "I'm on the tech side of things," which wasn't exactly true.

The super, a paunchy ex-rocker who kept his thinning hair shoulder-length and lustrous, shrugged and waved his hand in the air like someone trying to disperse a fart. "I meant it as a good thing. I hate those douchebags."

The elevator doors opened.

A silver skull with ruby eyes flickered from one of the super's manicured fingers as he pushed the button repeatedly. Did the machine sense the urgency? The irritation? Or was the super a speed freak? Both of his hands were adorned with rings. One looked like intertwined dragons breathing fire.

Neal counted the floors as the elevator ascended.

The doors opened on twenty-four, and Neal followed the super down the corridor, catching a faint whiff of some kind of pheromone-enhancing body spray, like something you'd use to cover up the stench of cat piss. The super stopped in front of an apartment and pulled out an electronic key card. He looked at Neal.

"Mr. LeBlanc doesn't stay here too much. I think he's got a girlfriend or something."

Neal nodded. "We just want to make sure he's okay."

The super used the key card, the lock spun, the door opened. Then the super, like all supers in the city, held out his hand so that Neal could grease his palm with a hundred-dollar bill.

"You want to come in with me?"

The super shook his head and stuck the bill into his pocket. "I'll be back in twenty. You find a body or something, just call 911."

The apartment was generic, like a suite in a Marriott. The draperies, the carpet, and the furniture were new and coordinated to appear tasteful and inoffensive.

Neal gave the bookshelves a quick scan. It was a meager collection, mostly business books and biographies of former presidents. You could tell a lot about a person from his bookshelves; these told Neal that LeBlanc didn't like to read.

He walked into the bedroom. Typically, if people had something to hide, they hid it there. LeBlanc's bedroom was even more boring than the living room.

Neal entered the master closet and saw a row of suits, a dozen variations of expensive blue and gray, dress shirts still wrapped in plastic from the dry cleaners, and a selection of striped ties. Freshly polished wing tips gleamed from the shoe rack. There wasn't a balled-up sock on the floor or a pair of tennis shoes.

Neal took out his iPhone and snapped a couple of photos. He pulled a pair of surgical gloves out of his pocket, slipped them on, and began opening drawers; he didn't want to compromise any evidence and, after years of experience, didn't want to touch anything yucky.

He carefully sifted through tie tacks, cuff links, socks, underwear, T-shirts, and unopened boxes of toiletries. There was nothing interesting. No concert ticket stubs, no condoms, no porno mags, no rolling papers, no sex toys.

Neal pulled a small flashlight from his sport coat and looked under the bed. There wasn't even a dust bunny.

The absence of luggage meant that LeBlanc was still on vacation, but after what they'd discovered in his accounts, Neal was pretty sure LeBlanc wasn't coming back.

A leather briefcase sat on the counter by the kitchen. He opened it and was unsurprised to see it was empty.

The kitchen cupboards were stocked with a few cans of soup, a jar of tomato sauce, boxes of dried pasta—the typical larder of someone who ate most of his meals at restaurants. According to the expiration date on a box of instant oatmeal, it had become inedible six months ago. Neal closed the cupboard and took off his gloves. He couldn't imagine anyone being such a neat freak. Had LeBlanc actually lived here?

On the refrigerator was a picture of LeBlanc, looking windswept and handsome, with his arm around a thin blond woman. They looked dressed for a garden party, designer sunglasses and hands clutching Aperol spritzes, like members of some kind of Long Island aristocracy. The beautiful people. The golden ones.

Neal plucked the photo off the fridge and stuck it into his pocket.

Bryan rolled off the woman and lay on his back, gasping. His chest heaved as he sucked in air as if he'd sprinted up four flights of stairs. He blinked sweat out of his eyes and turned toward her. She was lovely. Her deep brown skin was slick with sweat, her breasts spilling to one side, her eyes twinkling.

She laughed. "What happened to your nose, baby?"

He felt the condom clinging to his cock like a diaphanous stocking, but reached up and touched his nose. He'd gotten sunburnt on the ferry from Santo Domingo. It was nothing terrible, but enough to leave small flecks of skin detaching from his nose and forehead. "I'm peeling."

She laughed again. "White boys got to be careful in the sun." She had an amazing laugh, resonant and full.

He watched as she got out of bed and went into the bathroom. Bryan thought about his scrawny girlfriend in New York. When they had sex she'd be on top of him, lurching and flailing like one of those inflatable figures outside a used-car lot. It was frenetic and not always enjoyable. And the sounds she'd make, the screechy appeals to some higher power; they'd flattered him at the time, but now it all seemed like a phony porn-inspired performance designed to inflate the male ego. Couldn't people just fuck without turning it into some kind of showstopper?

This woman didn't do any of that.

The toilet flushed, the shower turned on. He felt he was getting a crash course in the Caribbean region. After he left the Dominican Republic, going to Puerto Rico was an easy and obvious first move. It was an incorporated part of the United States, and while Bryan didn't know what that meant legally for the Commonwealth of Puerto Rico, he did know that it meant an American could enter and exit without much fuss. He took the ferry from Santo Domingo to San Juan, and then hired a car service to drive him across the island to Fajardo.

In Fajardo he ate tostones and drank a Coquí lager. Then he boarded the fast ferry to St. Thomas in the US Virgin Islands, another unincorporated territory of the United States. How many unincorporated territories did the United States have? Bryan thought Guam probably fell into this category.

His itinerary hadn't been random. He'd spent hours in the New York Public Library using its computers—he knew they'd search his browser history at the office—to look up the various ferry routes and schedules, trying to figure out the most discreet way to travel across a group of islands. These moves were all part of his getaway plan. Any private detective the company might contract would pick up his trail and follow it to the Virgin Islands, but that's where the trail would grow cold. He was only in St. Thomas for a few hours, long enough to buy a few bottles of rum and to meet up with a nice Australian couple who were spending a year bouncing around the Caribbean on a sailboat. He'd connected with them through his sailing club's Facebook page and they were happy to give him a lift. He'd introduced himself as Randy, an advertising executive who'd been downsized and was spending his severance package traveling the world. He'd let his beard grow for the past week and thought he looked like a rich hipster on vacation. He told them his plan was to sit in a hammock and drink beer. His only desires were to feel the ocean breeze tickle his bare feet, never look at a spreadsheet again, and waste away in Margaritaville. Which was, more or less, the truth.

Bryan made sure to annoy the Australians by playing the Grateful Dead on their sound system whenever possible. If anyone ever asked, they'd say they gave an obnoxious Deadhead a ride to Jamaica, some dude who was going to the Reggae Sunsplash festival.

They docked in Ocho Rios, on the north side of Jamaica, and while the two Australians went to check in with the authorities and get their cruising permit, Bryan walked off the boat and into the city.

He'd asked a cabdriver for a quiet, inexpensive hotel, and the driver had taken him to a discreet two-star place that advertised itself as "unpretentious." It was just outside the city, flanked by an overgrown lot on one side and a small cluster of houses on the other. Bryan thought it was more ramshackle than unpretentious, but it was clean and perfect for his purpose. As he checked in, he spun a story for the hotel clerk about how he'd lost everything in a brutal divorce and didn't want his ex or her lawyer to find him. He needed to relax. Walk on the beach. Piece his life back together. He tried to look sad and ultimately convinced the clerk to register him as "Mr. Smith" by paying cash for a week in advance and slipping her an extra hundred-dollar bill.

The hotel clerk's name was Grace, and she had been intrigued by his story, or at least curious enough that a few days later she joined him for dinner and drinks and followed him back to his room. Casual sex hadn't really been part of Bryan's plans—not that he was opposed to it on moral or religious grounds—but a couple of days spent walking on the beach and sitting around the hotel had made him anxious.

Bryan gently pulled the condom off his cock and flicked it into a trash can as Grace came out of the bathroom. She stood naked at the end of the bed, drying her hair with a towel. Bryan couldn't help admiring her. She was relaxed and warm—the opposite of the kind of women he'd dated in the city, who were uptight and cold, like neurotic Popsicles.

"What're you doing today?" she asked.

Bryan shrugged. "Maybe go to the waterfall."

"Dunn's River?" Grace laughed. "Well, you have fun, but don't drink the water."

"Kids pee in it?"

"Kids aren't the problem." She pulled on her dress and smiled at him. "Well, Mr. Smith, I think you enjoyed yourself last night."

Bryan returned her smile. "Very much so."

She patted the bed. "Then show Grace your appreciation."

Bryan looked at her. He never liked it when people referred to themselves in the third person, and for a moment, he was unsure exactly what she was asking. Did she want a kiss? A snuggle? And then it dawned on him.

"Like a tip?"

She nodded. "Two hundred dollars should do."

It was a stupid postcard, the kind of thing a tourist would send. A vacation shot of a beautiful cocoa-skinned woman, her breasts packed into a teeny red-and-white bikini, her lips spread in a bright smile with glimmering, Photoshop-bleached teeth, as she cradled a bunch of bright green bananas in her arms. Behind her, palm trees swayed in the computer-enhanced sky and turquoise waves curled up against ecru sand; it was a beach that looked exotic and safe, hygienic Caribbean. A typographically jaunty font proclaimed GREETINGS FROM PUNTA CANA!

"The Dominican Republic?"

Neal could feel his allergies kicking up, the smoke from the woman's cigarette making him miserable. He was surprised LeBlanc would be involved with someone who smoked. But it was the right person, the skinny blonde in the photo he'd snagged off LeBlanc's fridge. Neal flipped the card over. There was her name and address. He chewed on his thumbnail for a moment, squinting at the fine print. She took a last drag and blew a thin stream toward his face as she stubbed her cigarette out in an ashtray. Neal slowly blinked, letting the smoke dissipate. He looked at the smashed cigarette butt and couldn't help noticing the vibrant red lipstick smears encircling it.

"We were supposed to go there on vacation. He'd bought two weeks at some all-inclusive resort."

"Why didn't you go with him?"

"Looks like I got dumped."

"Do you think he's still down there?"

"How the fuck should I know? My boyfriend took a luxury vacation and all I got was a stupid postcard."

It hadn't taken Neal long to track her down. A quick check of LeBlanc's office phone records and a hack of his Facebook account and here he was, getting a bitter raft of shit from an angry ex-girlfriend.

"Did he say anything before he left?"

"Like what?"

"Some hint of his intentions."

She narrowed her eyes. "He ghosted me."

"Ghosted you how?"

"Like a fucking ghost. How else do you do it?"

"The last time you saw him, did he behave differently?"

She shook her head. "He was as weird as always."

"Weird?"

"He was a weird dude." She lit another cigarette and blew smoke at him. "But he was great between the sheets."

Neal decided not to press; he might need to talk to her again and didn't want her to do anything like disappear or, worse, hire a publicist.

She looked nice enough, pretty in the way that rich white women from Connecticut are pretty, her blond hair pulled into a sporty ponytail, her body long and lean and dressed in something casual and expensive. He could see why LeBlanc had been attracted to her. She was the kind of woman the Wall Streeters were drawn to, finely tuned like a top-of-the-line Tesla. Neal guessed she played tennis and mixed a good Manhattan. Smoking appeared to be her only flaw.

He flipped the postcard back and forth. Besides the name and address, there was only one word scrawled on the message side of the postcard.

"*Mofongo?* What's that mean?"

"Maybe it means 'suck it' in Spanish." She tapped her ash into the ashtray and smirked. She smirked right to his face. "You know, when you called and told me what he did, I wasn't surprised. But I can't figure out how he got away with it. A whole office full of financial geniuses and he embezzles millions. How did he pull that off?"

Neal didn't answer. He hadn't wanted to tell her what LeBlanc had done, but she wouldn't talk to him otherwise.

"But now I know."

There was something in her voice, some subtle shade. Neal felt his face flush, felt his collar suddenly tighten. "What do you mean?"

She laughed, smoke popping out of her mouth in gray clumps. "You're just a bunch of fucking nerds."

As far as natural wonders go, Dunn's Falls was pretty good. Not awesome like Niagara Falls or Iguaçu Falls, and not breathtakingly beautiful like the thousand-foot waterfalls in Hawaii, but bigger than he'd expected, though not a roaring wall of water either. It was a comparatively laid-back waterfall.

But as far as tourist attractions go it was a madhouse. Human chains of pasty vacationers in swimsuits held hands as their Jamaican guides led them up the falls. Bryan didn't bother to count, but it looked like there were about two hundred people clambering through the water, trying to navigate the slippery rocks, while official photographers took photos and videos of them. That was the genius of the scheme: drag tourists through the water and then sell them pictures of themselves being dragged through the water. There was a lot of shouting and encouragement. The tourists were urged to get up, stand up, stand up on the rocks. It was a strange thing to watch. Everyone was splashing and slipping and getting drenched. They seemed genuinely happy, as if the water pouring off the mountain was filled with some kind of wonder drug.

Maybe that was the thing. If you don't have much, you need to invent ways to make money, need to think outside the box and turn a perfectly nice but unremarkable waterfall into a tourist attraction. And not just a pleasant place where you charge an entrance fee: You employ dozens of locals to act as guides to lead the tourists through the water and photographers to sell souvenir photos. You sell T-shirts and tchotchkes, Jamaican beef patties and Red Stripe beer. Bryan smiled to himself. It was a bit like Grace asking for a tip. It wasn't that she was a prostitute; she was just thinking of ways to augment her income. He found himself admiring her for it. Just like Dunn's Falls, it was about being creative.

Bryan decided to take Grace's advice and stay out of the water. Instead he bought a cold beer and sat on a bench, watching the tourists ascend the falls.

He wondered if it said something about him. Why didn't he feel like putting on his swimsuit and jumping in with the rest of humanity? He realized he'd always been like that. He'd drifted through adolescence without ever becoming a Boy Scout or playing football; he never joined a club or a committee or a gang in high school. He didn't feel like making a commitment to an organized anything. He didn't want to be labeled. He wasn't a Democrat or a Republican or a member of the Democratic Socialists. He could barely be bothered to vote.

His friends from college were all off living their lives, getting married and raising little kids. He didn't see them much anymore.

Bryan watched a young woman in a bikini slip on the rocks and fall under the water. She emerged with a grin on her face and let out a whoop. He drained the rest of his beer and tossed the empty bottle into a trash can. A friendly Jamaican man asked if he'd like his picture taken by the waterfall, but Bryan shook his head. All these people having fun were getting him down.

Seo-yun had just wrapped her lips around the tip of his penis when her phone started vibrating and a ringtone erupted from the bedside table. She didn't need to look. It was her fiancé. He'd chosen a special ringtone for his calls. Seo-yun didn't think you could find a more annoying song than Atlantic Starr singing "Always," but that's what he'd stuck on her phone. He said it was the most popular first dance song at weddings. He was looking forward to that first dance and had even scheduled lessons with a choreographer to help them come up with something fun and memorable that they could video and put online. Apparently that was a thing people did.

Recently he'd been calling and texting nonstop, bugging her about the invitations, wanting to work on the custom vows he'd insisted on writing, double-checking with her about the flowers, the venue, the menu, her dress. Shouldn't she pick out her own dress? Did she have to hear that song fifty times a day?

The air in the room caused a shiver to bloom across her skin, but it felt nice to be naked, to pull off her skirt and blouse and reveal her lean body. She let her tongue roll lazily around the end of the young man's penis and felt him shudder. Maybe she'd tell her fiancé to include a line in the vows where she promised to be faithful unless he irritated the shit out of her and she felt like fucking someone on her lunch hour.

The song began playing again and the guy said, "Do you need to get that?"

Seo-yun shook her head and continued exploring his cock with her mouth.

"You sure?"

"Mm-hmm."

As she sucked his cock, Seo-yun realized that this was just another part of foreign exchange. Bodies got together and swapped value in what one hoped was an equitable exchange. Although she knew it wasn't uncommon among her male colleagues, this was the first time Seo-yun had taken someone to a hotel for sex, maybe even the first time she'd ducked out of the office in the middle of the afternoon for any reason. It was completely out of character.

His name was Stanford—like the university in California—and he was the grandson of one of the board members at the firm. Stanford, a twenty-five-year-old with a brand-new MBA and a silver spoon in his mouth, was sent to see her about working on the forex desk. It wasn't your typical entry-level position in financial services. Stanford would not be starting at the bottom.

He was interested in foreign exchange, and Seo-yun was told to show him the ropes, to see if he would be a good fit in her department. He was smart, obviously, and earnest, but he wasn't shy, and she felt some instant sexual tension between them. Normally she would've ignored it, but her phone kept ringing, her fiancé kept texting, and it started to get under her skin. So she invited him out to lunch. Why she did it, she couldn't say exactly. It was impulsive and it turned her on.

This kind of thing could be dangerous.

When she'd looked at his résumé, she discovered that he had been selected all-state lacrosse in his undergrad days, and she hadn't been disappointed when he peeled off his shirt to reveal a well-toned body. She couldn't remember the last time she touched clearly defined abs. Would it kill her fiancé to hit the gym a few times a week?

She moved her head back and forth, taking his shaft in deeply, then pulling back and rolling her tongue along the tip, slurping up her saliva, getting his cock thoroughly lubricated.

It wasn't professional of her to do this. HR wouldn't approve. But then she was probably going to be unemployed soon, taking the fall for Bryan's embezzlement. That was what happened when you gave someone your trust. There was a meeting with the chief executive scheduled at four that afternoon, and she liked the idea that she'd get fired stinking of illicit sex.

Her cell phone sang again. She felt the young man shift his stance. She looked up and blinked at him. "It's only my fiancé."

"What?"

"My fiancé. He wants me to look at some napkins or something."

The young man paused—she could tell he was thinking about some comforting thing to say or maybe an exit strategy— but he just nodded and said, "Okay."

She began stroking him in earnest, sucking the tip and jacking his shaft until he started to come. She pulled her face back and let his semen shoot all over her neck and breasts. She looked up at him. He seemed surprised. Seo-yun smeared his come around her breasts, the sticky fluid coating her nipples. She stood up and kissed him. "Now let's see you apply for that job." And with that she lay on the bed and waited for him to return the favor.

Neal leaned back into the worn vinyl seat of the yellow cab as it slalomed through the city. His office was downtown and, theoretically, he could have walked to the subway, maybe gotten some of the awful woman's smoke off his clothes, but taking a cab gave him a chance to think. Neal's job at InterFund was called "special collections." He was a one-person department whose job was tracking down investors who'd overreached, taken bad bets, had their margins called, and then skipped out. It did not typically mean going after someone who worked at the company, especially not someone like Bryan LeBlanc.

It didn't make a lot of sense to Neal. LeBlanc had been a rising star at InterFund, handpicked and groomed for leadership by the CEO himself and destined to become a managing director of the foreign exchange division. He was handsome, friendly, and liked by everyone. If he'd stayed the course, he would've been pulling a seven-figure salary in a couple of years. A multimillionaire by the time he was forty. Wasn't that why these guys got into the business in the first place? Why rip off the company?

There was no evidence of what Neal called the "big three," the typical reasons that led to this kind of behavior. These were: drug abuse, usually cocaine or some variety of prescription painkillers; getting in too deep with a bookie by betting on the Jets, Mets, or Nets; or an addiction to expensive prostitutes. So far he'd come up with nothing.

LeBlanc had faked documents that gave him permission to borrow against his clients' funds and invest the money on their behalf. Normally there was nothing unusual about this—lots of traders invested in margin funds; they just had their client's permission. When the market was performing and stocks were rising, a good investor could double, even triple his money playing the margin. When the market dropped, well, that was no fun for anyone.

LeBlanc had run the money through an elaborate string of bogus bank accounts and foreign exchange manipulations, making thousands of trades, some lasting less than a couple of seconds. Neal could hardly follow the trail—the world of foreign exchange was unregulated and more like the Wild West than like any other branch of the financial services industry.

When the market was hot, no one cared; on paper it looked as if investors were making money. LeBlanc's scheme was discovered only when the British pound devalued overnight, the market adjusted, and one of his institutional clients did an audit.

By then, LeBlanc and $17 million had Houdinied to parts unknown.

That was another thing that puzzled Neal. Why didn't LeBlanc take more? He had access to it. Bernie Madoff had pocketed billions. Why so little?

As the cab lurched up to his office he caught a glimpse of himself in the taxi's rearview mirror. LeBlanc's girlfriend had called him a nerd. It was true that his skin was pale and, even though he had turned thirty-three, he still suffered from occasional breakouts of ragged pink acne. In his mind, nerds were smart people who lacked style. But he had style. He had cool glasses. His hair was pushed into a shapeless ridge in the middle of his head, something his stylist called a faux hawk. And he didn't wear the typical navy pin-striped uniform of his fellow investment bankers. He wasn't a nerd; he was a rebel in chukka boots.

Neal strolled into InterFund's office—all steel and glass and security cameras—and nodded to the guards. He swiped his ID card to access the elevator, punched the button for the eleventh floor, and watched the LED stock ticker read out prices in real time as he ascended.

He walked through the open office plan, past the dozens of traders staring intently at monitors, and unlocked his door and entered his office. Neal felt fortunate that he wasn't stuck in some cubicle, but then he was afforded privacy because he dealt with sensitive issues and information, things that the company did not want showing up in the *Wall Street Journal* or, worse, on a gossipy website.

He stuck the postcard—GREETINGS FROM PUNTA CANA!—on the corkboard above his desk. He had slipped it into his pocket and, honestly, he didn't feel bad about stealing it from LeBlanc's smoky girlfriend. If he'd asked to keep it she would've said no just to be an asshole. Neal sat down at his computer, entered his password, and began googling. He didn't know what he was looking for, but sift through enough raw data—someone's credit card statement, for example—and you usually find a pattern.

When a margin is called, the bank seizes the account to cover the losses. This is legal. It's in the fine print at the bottom of your account agreement. Neal thought more people should read that before they began speculating. However, if the client loses more than what's in the account—not uncommon with people engaged in commodities speculation—the bank will put a lien on any real estate the client might own or force the sale of art collections, automobiles, and boats. Basically anything the client had of value would be seized. Of course, not all clients feel like paying up; sometimes they go on the run, and that's where Neal came in. Special collections was like a cross between a private detective and repo man, and Neal enjoyed the work. The human stories were interesting—there was always an explanation for not paying the bank—and he liked the challenge of tracking people down. In typical cases, he could find people quickly. Even if they'd sold their house and abandoned their car and were living with an old college chum, he could track them down. There were the obvious, sloppy mistakes. It could be a Facebook page or a Twitter account, a Tinder profile or an Instagram feed. Sometimes they'd skip town and leave a forwarding address with the post office. A large percentage moved back to their parents' house. More often than not they stayed home and kept going to their jobs like nothing was unusual, as if they hadn't lost a gamble on the stock market and seen their nest egg vanish; they just didn't answer the phone calls, emails, and certified letters the collections department sent. Ostriches, he called them. These types of cases usually took only a couple of hours to close. He'd find them, get an arrest warrant or a court order seizing their property, and have the local sheriff pick them up. Once these ostriches were in police custody they were surprisingly eager to reach a settlement. Most of the time people seemed relieved to be found. They wouldn't have to hide forever; they could face the consequences and get their life back. Neal didn't have a degree in psychology, nor had he ever studied criminal pathology, but in his experience he'd learned that the human brain craves order, and the guilty seek justice even if it's not in their best interest. It's just the way people are wired.

But if they actively went underground, well, that was different. That required some legwork. He'd get a court order and freeze their accounts. That usually did the trick. When someone no longer has access to his bank accounts, credit cards, cell phones, etc., he gets a lawyer and starts trying to make a deal pretty quickly. Not a lot of people store cash under their mattress. Although, given how unstable the markets were, it didn't seem like the worst place to park some assets.

But this case was different. This guy knew how the system worked, and he had a head start and $17 million.

Neal hoped LeBlanc had some kind of kink. In a perfect world, Neal would find LeBlanc bound and ball-gagged by a dominatrix in a luxury hotel suite somewhere in the Dominican Republic. All he had to do was contact the fancy hotels and resorts in the area and inquire about big cash transactions. That might take him a week, maybe two. If he was lucky, he'd have to expend a little shoe leather on the case, maybe even catch a few hours in a hammock on the beach. He couldn't remember the last time he'd taken a vacation.

Neal liked to work in a methodical way. He didn't want to waste time chasing shadows or hunches, so he decided to start at the last known location of Mr. Bryan LeBlanc. Punta Cana was, according to Wikipedia, a resort city on the easternmost tip of the Dominican Republic with "one of the busiest and best connected airports in the Caribbean." He was about to call the Punta Cana Airport's security office when his in-house messenger and his iPhone beeped simultaneously. Both messages were marked "Urgent." He was needed in the CEO's office immediately.

As he got off the elevator, Neal popped two curiously strong peppermints into his mouth and considered what he should and shouldn't tell his superiors. There wasn't a lot to go on, but it wasn't what he would call a dead end. Unless the person commits suicide or dies in an accident, there is no such thing as a dead end, and even then he'd heard rumors that Kenneth Lay, the pirate captain who scuttled Enron, had faked his death and was living on an island somewhere.

The CEO's executive assistant pointed to the door. "They're expecting you."

Neal pushed through the door and felt the unmistakable embrace of wealth and power wrap around him. It was like entering another world. The air smelled different, as if it had been filtered through the Swiss Alps. Even the light was different; it was soft, luxurious even, designed to make clients feel like the millions of bucks they were entrusting to the bank.

The CEO stood and reached toward him. "Good to see you, Cornelius; thanks for coming on such short notice."

The CEO was the only person, besides his parents, who called him by his legal name. When Neal asked his parents why they gave him that name, they just laughed and told him they liked watching *Soul Train*. As if it were a hilarious joke to name your son after an emcee—a side effect, he realized, of his parents' deep fondness for marijuana. He'd gone by Neal since high school.

Neal felt the well-practiced handshake the CEO proffered. The chief executive looked older than when he'd seen him a few months ago; the steel-blue eyes still coordinated with his tie, but they were behind thick glasses now, and the butter-rich lunches at four-star restaurants had finally caught up with him. According to the office grapevine, the CEO had developed a nasty case of gout and was no longer able to play tennis on the weekends, so his tan had faded and he'd developed a paunch and a rubbery double chin. He looked like just another overeducated, underexercised white-collar worker.

Neal turned and saw Seo-yun Kim, the managing director on the foreign exchange desk. She sat on the edge of the sofa looking nervous.

The CEO pointed at the couch, indicating he should sit. Neal sat down next to her.

"How's the LeBlanc case coming?"

Neal had expected a bit of small talk, maybe an introduction. But the CEO didn't seem to be in the mood to waste any time. Neal decided to do the same. "I think we should get the FBI involved. We've got a clear-cut case of embezzlement. This is what the FBI does best."

The CEO took off his glasses and cleaned them with a tissue. It reminded Neal of an actor doing something to appear thoughtful. Neal watched Seo-yun watching the CEO. She sat very still, her eyes focused. Neal sniffed the air. She was wearing a musky perfume. Neal leaned closer and inhaled deeply, trying to place the scent radiating from her body. She turned her head and gave him a strange look.

The CEO put his glasses back on and cleared his throat. "It would cause irreparable harm to the firm if this went public. I've already spoken to the board, and we all agree that we deal with this in-house. Are you up to it?"

Neal leaned forward. "Two weeks ago he left the country. No one's seen him since."

The CEO made a sour face. "So he could be anywhere?"

Neal nodded. "Apparently he bought one of those prepaid, all-inclusive trips to a resort."

"Where is this resort?"

"The Dominican Republic."

The CEO was silent for a moment, and then he spoke. He said the word slowly. *"Mo-ther-fucker."*

Neal continued. "He left the resort and from there he could jump to all kinds of safe havens: Brazil, the Caymans, Venezuela. He could be anywhere."

Seo-yun broke her silence. "He created a very complex string of transactions to hide the money. We're trying to unravel it."

The CEO rubbed his face with his hands. "I hired him. I promoted him. I championed that shithead. You understand what I'm saying?"

"I'll need to hire some outside consultants." Neal then pointed at Seo-yun. "And I'll need her. I don't really understand how forex works."

"Nobody does. That's why we make so much money from it."

Seo-yun looked at Neal. "I'll help in any way I can."

The CEO cleared his throat. "Good. Both of you do whatever it is you do. He ripped off some important clients, people who could make this a very public scandal. If you need to hire some foot soldiers, some mercenaries, do it. I don't care what it costs. Find this asshole, I don't want him to get a penny of the money he stole. Find him and bring his ass back in a sling. Just don't let anyone know what you're doing and for fuck's sake don't bring law enforcement into it."

They left the CEO's office, the plush carpet giving way to shiny faux terrazzo. A soft robotic chime announced the arrival of the lift, and when the doors opened, they entered. They stood in the elevator side by side, watching the numbers count down.

Seo-yun handed Neal her business card. "Anything you want me to do, let me know. I feel terrible about what happened."

He took the card. "It's not your fault."

"That's not the perception."

Neal leaned close to her and inhaled. She turned her head. "Do you have allergies or something?"

Neal blushed. "I'm just trying to figure out what kind of perfume you're wearing."

Seo-yun smiled. "It's come."

The elevator doors opened and Seo-yun walked off. As they closed Neal wondered if she meant come like semen or Cum like some brand of perfume he'd never heard of.

The farther they got from shore, the stronger the fishing boat's cargo began to smell; the salty tang of freshly caught sea creatures mixed with the scent of burning cannabis. Bryan turned and saw the captain—his rank signified by a weather-beaten captain's hat perched on top of a pile of dreadlocks—sitting in the cockpit with one hand on the wheel, steering the little fishing boat across the open water. The copilot, a strikingly handsome young man, sat next to the captain, a burning spliff dangling from his lips. He leaned his head back and exhaled, the smoke drifting past Bryan and out over the open water.

Bryan blinked. It was a cliché, right? Like in that movie, *The Harder They Come.*

The boat wasn't big, maybe a twenty-five-footer, and while the captain and his copilot enjoyed the shade of the cockpit, Bryan sat on a large cooler, broiling in the afternoon sun. There were nine, maybe ten coolers, the biggest he'd ever seen, filled with queen conch, a giant sea snail that you could harvest only with a special government-sanctioned permit. Naturally the captain didn't have a special permit and so was taking his bootleg haul two hundred miles across the water to the Cayman Islands.

The copilot took a long inhale of the spliff and then glanced back at Bryan. "You want a taste?"

Bryan nodded and walked up to the cockpit. He wasn't much of a stoner, having smoked only occasionally with some of the people at the sailing club, but it was an excuse to get out of the sun. He took a hit and tasted an earthy, sweet flavor in the back of his throat. Bryan coughed. He looked at the captain. "You don't smoke?"

The captain shook his head, and the copilot laughed. "He don't do nothing. No ganja, no alcohol. He's a vegan."

The captain scowled. "I'm straightedge, is what I am. I like to be healthy."

The copilot laughed again. "I like to be healthy too. That's why I wear a condom when I'm selling sugarcane to the tourists."

The captain turned to Bryan and said, "He sapps."

"What's that?"

"He's a gigolo. A man prostitute."

The copilot flicked the end of the spliff out into the water. "I work in the hospitality and tourism sector of the Jamaican economy, and I am not happy sitting out here with a load of ass-reeking conch."

Bryan smiled. "A gigolo? What's that like?"

The copilot leaned in close to Bryan. "Single women come to the island looking for some sun, some fun, and some cockie. Am I right?"

Bryan nodded. "I suppose so."

"Everybody wants to have sex with a Jamaican. You probably paid for a little duggu-duggu while you were here." The copilot chuckled.

Bryan felt his face flush. It was true, he had paid for sex, although it was an inadvertent after-the-fact kind of sex-for-hire. He wouldn't have slept with Grace if he'd known she was going to ask for money. Although he didn't regret paying. Maybe he was just doing his part for the Jamaican economy.

"Being an escort is a good gig, man. I look right in their eyes, give 'em some of that 'Hakuna Matata' stuff they like, maybe smoke a little with them, and the next thing they are paying to suck my dick."

The captain shook his head. "That ain't what I heard."

The copilot told Bryan, "He's just jealous 'cause he's driving this tub of conch 'stead of drinking Chardonnay with a white girl."

The captain laughed. "The conch will be here longer than your good looks."

"What about you?" the copilot asked Bryan. "Why are you skulking about on a rickety old tub?"

"My ex got everything in the divorce. So I took off. Trying to find myself or something like that."

"Any luck?" the captain asked.

"I'm feeling better."

The copilot burst out howling. "Maybe you can learn to dive for conch. Get a whole new career."

The captain shook his head. "Better you keep runnin' from your wife."

Bryan thought it was strange that these two men were so eager to share their criminal occupations. Was this what criminals did when they got together? Was he supposed to tell them what he'd done? He was relieved when the conversation turned to a spirited debate on the skills of a snooker player named Rory McLeod. The captain was a fan; the copilot was not.

Bryan wondered how he got himself into a life of crime. He'd only pulled off his scheme because crime was scalable. Criminals stole what they had access to. The captain had access to conch. The copilot—and Bryan recognized that prostitution wasn't technically stealing—had access to horny women. Because he was a white man with a college degree, Bryan had been put in a position of trust that gave him access to millions of dollars. Given the same opportunities, would the captain or the copilot do what he'd done? Somehow he doubted it. They were criminals out of necessity, while he was more of a philosophical criminal. He wanted to give the system a taste of its own medicine. But now he wondered if it even noticed.

Bryan closed his eyes and let the ganja and the boat rock him to sleep. As he drifted off he wondered if this was going to be his life now: moving in the criminal underworld, sleeping with one eye open, never sure whom he could trust, always looking over his shoulder. For the first time it occurred to him that maybe he wasn't cut out to spend his life riding around in rickety fishing boats laden with contraband gastropods.

Seo-yun stood behind the breakfast bar in her open-plan kitchen and stared at the microwave.

Her fiancé sat at the dining room table holding two different wedding invitations side by side. He seemed to be thinking awfully hard about it.

The microwave beeped and she took her frozen dinner out. She stirred the noodles in her vegan pad Thai and tasted it. No spice hit her tongue, no bright flavor exploded in her mouth. It was a kind of tomatoey mush, low cal and convenient, another bland cop-out. The story of her life. Like this wedding.

Seo-yun thought about LeBlanc. In some ways she envied him. She wished she could say fuck it and go off and create a whole new life. Not that she would steal from the company to do it—she wasn't a crook. In fact she was the opposite of a crook. Crooks were daring. Then, on second thought, she'd been daring with a young lacrosse player that afternoon, so maybe she did have a taste for a little transgression. Was it a crime to rebel? Did it hurt anyone for her to let some spontaneity into her life? She thought she would feel guilty, but instead she felt disconnected, as if she was having an out-of-body experience. Not during the sex part. That part was an in-the-body experience, but it was her reaction in the aftermath that felt so strange.

Perhaps it was because she'd played it safe her entire life. From elementary school through to her MBA, she'd always done what she was told and excelled at everything she did. According to her parents and friends and society she should be happy. And on many levels she was happy. She enjoyed her work, loved living in the city, spent her discretionary income traveling; she had it all. So why was she feeling the need to act out? Why couldn't she revel in the glow of corporate success? Maybe it was a deeper, spiritual itch that needed scratching, something that Cardio Barre classes weren't really getting at. Or perhaps she needed to go wild for a weekend, go to Vegas and do whatever people did there or fly out to Burning Man, drop acid, and get gangbanged in the orgy dome. She'd read an article about that. "Transcendent," one participant said.

Her fiancé looked up at her. "I'm not sure about the Helvetica. I know it's modern but, I don't know, it seems like we're announcing a merger and acquisition," he said.

Seo-yun smiled and then, after a thoughtful pause, said, "Do you think it would be all right if I occasionally hooked up with random guys?"

Her fiancé looked confused. "What?"

"For sex," she clarified.

He put down the wedding invitations. "But we're going to be married."

Seo-yun nodded. "That's why I'm asking. Would it bother you?"

His lips blew into a pout. "Yes. Yes, I think it would."

Seo-yun scooped another clump of bland noodles into her mouth.

"Why? Is it something you want to do?"

She shrugged. "I just want to know what's expected."

He reached out across the breakfast bar and touched her hand. "I know it's normal to get cold feet before doing something like this. It's a big commitment. A lifetime commitment."

She let his hand linger. He smiled at her.

"Soy, if you need more time or you want to talk things through or you want to go to couples therapy, whatever you need, I'm here for you."

Seo-yun appreciated his offer. But how could she explain that the life he'd envisioned was so completely normal that it seemed like something he'd pulled off the shelf at IKEA? It was an impulse-free, fun-deficient life devoid of imagination; there was no space for wildness, for eccentricity, or for originality. It made her throat feel tight. Seo-yun withdrew her hand. "I like the Helvetica."

"Really?"

She put her hands on her hips in a clear signal that she was serious and nodded. "I've got to do some work."

He scoffed. "The markets are closed."

"I've been put on a special case."

"You make it sound like you're an FBI agent or something."

She smiled condescendingly. "I can neither confirm nor deny. Top secret."

"Oh, don't be like that." He stood and wrapped his arms around her from behind. "I was kidding." He put his face close to her neck and took a deep inhale. "Wow. You smell good."

Seo-yun unlocked his fingers from around her waist and walked into the bedroom and opened her computer.

Criminals weren't particularly trustworthy. That much was clear to Bryan. After all, they made their living breaking rules, taking what wasn't theirs, and betraying people's trust. A religious person might say that criminals were evil, but that seemed a bit of a stretch. He wasn't evil. Maybe *shameful* was a better word. Then again, maybe it wasn't just criminals; maybe no one was trustworthy. If you bought into capitalism as an economic system, a system designed to fuck over the majority of the populace for the benefit of the few, then you were putting your faith in something that was created to rip you off if you didn't rip the other guy off first. American society was based on this kind of opportunistic treachery and deceit.

Bryan figured that if he could rip off his employer, then it stood to reason that his coconspirator, an assistant bank manager named Leighton, might just as easily rip him off. But what choice did he have? He had to trust someone. He had to move the money out of an electronically traceable account and put it into a place where an injunction or bank order couldn't find it and freeze it. But once you move from digital money to analog money it's vulnerable to theft. It was so much money anyone would be tempted. What's the world coming to when an embezzler gets embezzled?

Despite the name, Grand Cayman was a small island, and George Town was what passed for a big city on a small island. Most of the businesses were on South Church Street, the main tourist strip that ran along the waterfront. The Jamaican conch delivery had taken place at a private dock on the other side of the island, and Bryan had managed to catch a ride with the truck driver who was delivering the contraband to restaurants in George Town—not that the chefs knew the conch had been illegally harvested. They just knew it was fresh.

Bryan sat at a table in a restaurant waiting for his Cayman contact. The restaurant was, oddly enough, across the street from a Harley-Davidson dealership. Why would someone buy a motorcycle on a small island? The restaurant was nice, not too fancy, but tastefully decorated with pictures of boats and a large taxidermy fish of some kind mounted above the bar. Best of all, it was filled with tourists from a cruise ship. No one would know Bryan and his contact; no one would even remember they were here.

Bryan was hungry, so he ordered conch fritters and a pint of Caybrew lager while he waited. This would be the moment of truth. Would his man show up? If he'd gotten burned, he didn't know what he'd do. He'd heard that criminals want to get caught, that they want to be punished because it makes living with the guilt easier. But Bryan didn't want to get punished. Fuck that. He had a few thousand dollars in his backpack. What were his options? Become a drifter? A homeless beach bum? Get a job waiting tables? Maybe he could save up and buy a Harley. Then he could ride around the island, letting the wind sting his skin and the sun bake his brain until he went totally insane and rode off a cliff.

Leighton arrived a few minutes late. Bryan remembered him from the one time they'd met: a skinny guy with light brown skin, close-cropped hair, and thick horn-rimmed glasses. He was wearing crisply pressed slacks and a pale yellow polo shirt—the kind that annoyed Bryan, the kind with the little animal embroidered on the chest. Leighton extended his hand and Bryan shook it. He wasn't sure how to act in this situation. Were they business partners meeting for the first time? Were they old friends? Was anyone watching?

Leighton slid into the chair opposite Bryan and handed him a manila envelope. Bryan noticed that Leighton's hands were shaking. He didn't know if it was reassuring that his contact was as nervous as he was or if it meant something was about to go south.

Leighton took the napkin and dabbed his forehead. "Did you have a good journey?"

"It's been interesting."

Bryan opened the envelope and saw a set of keys, a couple of documents, and a new passport. The passport was bright red with a regal-looking crest embossed in the center, framed by a lion and unicorn. "Is that a unicorn?"

Leighton nodded. "Part of the British royal family crest, I believe."

Bryan noticed that it was a British and Cayman Islands passport. "Does this make me a British citizen?"

Leighton mopped his forehead again. "Absolutely."

Bryan grinned. "How did that happen?"

"We are allowed to issue emergency passports here. You just have to know the right people."

"And be willing to pay."

Leighton turned his palms up. "Of course."

Bryan opened the passport and saw his face grinning back from the photo. It was a photo he'd had taken at the FedEx store in midtown and had sent to Leighton a few months ago. Then he looked at his new name. "Cuffy Ebanks?"

"It's a common name."

"Cuffy?"

"Ebanks is common. But this name will not raise any eyebrows. You'll be one of us."

Bryan let the name roll around in his brain for a moment. *Cuffy.* It did have a kind of breezy, offhand quality. He wondered if a new name would change his life. Maybe he would become friendlier, transform into a jovial rum-sodden sailor named Cuffy, a fun-loving guy who skipped around the islands skinny-dipping with beautiful women and eating fresh fish all day.

Leighton leaned in and said, "There are the keys and a prepaid one-year lease as you requested. Everything in your new name. There is also a driver's license, and you have a healthy account at Butterfield Bank with a Visa card to match. Everything is handled like you asked. I noted the expenses on the spreadsheet."

"Thanks. Excellent work."

"Everything else is waiting for you in the condo." The conch fritters arrived and Leighton raised an eyebrow. "You like conch?"

Bryan didn't honestly know if he liked it or not, so he popped one into his mouth and chewed. It was delicious. Maybe Cuffy liked conch fritters; maybe they were his favorite food. "You want one?"

Leighton shook his head and fidgeted with his silverware. "I hope you enjoy your stay in Grand Cayman."

Bryan washed the conch down with his cold beer. "After this, it's probably better that you and I don't know each other."

Leighton smiled. "True."

"Did you take your commission?"

"I am all paid for. Thank you."

"And you're happy?"

"Extremely happy for the opportunity to serve you. If you need anything in the future, don't hesitate to reach out." With that Leighton stood and extended his hand. "Have a pleasurable life."

Bryan shook his hand and watched Leighton go out the door. Bryan wiped his palm on his napkin. That had to be the clammiest handshake he'd ever encountered. Why was Leighton so nervous?

Bryan ordered a second Caybrew. He didn't know what, but something felt a little off. He decided on a plan B, just in case. That was something his father had always teased him about: *The financial markets could crash tomorrow, and then what're you going to do?* Bryan had laughed at the time, told his dad he'd teach math at a community college or something noble like that. But this time, his father was right.

The first thing was to try out his new identity and credit card. He paid for lunch at the restaurant as Cuffy Ebanks. The card was not declined. Bryan then took a cab to the airport and rented a midsize car with a large trunk. He found an internet café and searched on Airbnb for a safe house. He wanted to be outside George Town and booked a little cottage on Seven Mile Beach. Even if he didn't use it, having a place to lie low gave him a boost of confidence.

He didn't know why he felt so skittish. Maybe the paranoia was all in his head; maybe it was because he was so close to the finish line. But then he remembered a favorite saying: "Just because you're paranoid doesn't mean they're not out to get you."

The condo was a new building with amenities like central air and a gated ground-floor parking garage, but it was built in the style of older island architecture, like a vintage mansion, with wide verandas and balconies on every level. It was well located, near the center of town, not far from the restaurant where he'd met Leighton. Bryan parked the car in the garage. As he got out he took a look around. There were only a couple of cars, but he couldn't help feeling he was being watched. It was a strange sensation. Something he'd never felt before.

He went up to the second floor, found his front door, and slid the key into the lock.

The condo was decorated in pastel pinks and seafoam greens, colors that accentuated the vibrant blue of the water across the street. Bryan thought about how he might furnish the place. Get some rattan furniture with tropical print cushions. Maybe buy a Rousseau and hang it in the living room.

Bryan opened the French doors and walked out onto the balcony. He could see George Town, a cruise ship in the harbor, the ocean beyond. Bryan had to admit that it was nice—he was sure Cuffy would've liked to stay a while—but putting down roots was not part of the plan. He'd stay in George Town only for a few days, pick up the money, and get off the island. The condo was another misdirection, just in case they somehow tracked him to the Caymans and found this address, which the police or whoever could stake out until his lease expired. By then, he'd be long gone.

He found the money neatly stacked in twelve nylon duffel bags in the bedroom closet. He knelt down and began unzipping them. It was all there: brick upon brick upon brick of currency, enough to build a wall to keep the world away. It was a miracle, really. He was surprised that he didn't feel like dumping it all out on the floor and rolling in it. After all this time spent juggling numbers, building a maze of digits connected to digits—all of it ephemeral, the ghost in the machine—it had never seemed real. Now it did. He didn't even feel like counting it. There was just too much.

It took him six trips, but he eventually got everything down the elevator and into his rental car.

He went back upstairs to the condo still feeling strange, like something wasn't quite right. Perhaps having all this cash was freaking him out. He looked out over the balcony, down at the street below. There was a guy sitting in a yellow Jeep reading a magazine. Was he watching him?

Even though a light rain had begun to fall, Bryan left the balcony door open and the lights on. He went down to the garage and, making sure to go in the opposite direction from the Jeep, quietly drove to the little beach cottage on the outskirts of town.

The music was so loud it rattled his teeth.

A muscular man named Brandon shouted into a microphone, urging those in the room to visualize the body they wanted. Neal tried to visualize himself as some kind of elite athlete, a gymnast maybe, with bulging muscles and an ass you could bounce a quarter off, but with the music thumping and disco lights pulsing and all that encouragement, it was difficult to concentrate on anything other than pedaling as fast as he could. Perhaps that was the point. Sweat dripped into his eyes and he cranked up the resistance, following Brandon's admonitions, trusting that "You're not going to die!" and "You got this!" were more than just reassurances, that they were some kind of prophecy, that he had some kind of control over his life as long as he kept pedaling.

Ever since the breakup with Bart, Neal would leave the office and take a spin class or a yoga class or go to a public talk or a wine tasting—something healthy or with personal growth possibilities—anything to avoid going back to his apartment. As if sweat or exhaustion or the endorphin rush would somehow erase the heartache he felt. Doing things and being active kept him from feeling sorry for himself. At least temporarily.

A cab deposited him at the corner of Twenty-Fourth and Tenth, and Neal shuffled down the block toward his building with a feeling of dread, which was strange because his apartment was in a well-maintained walk-up and the space was adorable. He liked his neighbors. The landlord was friendly and attentive. It was all kinds of perfect. Dread is a strange feeling.

He entered his apartment and put his bag down on the couch Bart had made him buy. He sighed. He'd blown thousands of dollars on this masterpiece of design, which Bart had wanted more than anything else, in the hope that they would turn it into some kind of sex platform, an extension of the bedroom, so that their lust could erupt in every room. At the very least Bart could give him a hand job while they sat on the three-hundred-dollar-a-yard fabric. But that didn't happen, and like the dream of being some kind of ripped and muscular athlete, it was just a fantasy. Instead of wanting hot sex, Bart sat on the couch watching baseball games and drinking beer. Not that there was anything wrong with being a sports fan. Who doesn't like sports? But after a few months of hearing Ron Darling and Keith Hernandez talk about the good old days, Neal began to feel that Bart was more interested in the Mets than in their relationship. As it turned out, he wasn't wrong. After two years together, Bart departed for sportier shores, shacking up with a lumbersexual rock-climbing instructor in Brooklyn.

Neal kicked off his shoes and shuffled into the bedroom. He hung up his jacket, draped his pants over the end of the bed, and tossed his sweaty clothes into the hamper. He pulled on an old T-shirt and some house pants. He didn't feel comfortable walking around his apartment naked, not like the amateur astronomer who lived across the street and spent his evenings naked at his window looking through a telescope.

Neal opened the drawer where he kept the take-out menus and spread them on the little bar that separated the kitchen from the living room. Noodle bowls, tacos, maybe something healthy like grilled salmon—none of it appealed to him. Eventually he settled on an order of sushi rolls. He cracked a beer—his favorite, a Bell's Oarsman—and opened his laptop.

Neal had asked compliance and the HR department to send him everything they had on LeBlanc and he had gotten a printout of LeBlanc's email traffic from the IT department. He'd asked for saved and deleted emails and the stack was bigger than he'd imagined.

LeBlanc had all the typical credentials: a membership in Alpha Kappa Psi, an MBA from Carnegie Mellon, an internship with Goldman Sachs; his first job was on the currency risk management team at JPMorgan. This was where LeBlanc made a name for himself. He had become, if the clipping from the *Wall Street Journal* was to be believed, an expert on something called passive currency hedging.

The intercom buzzed, and though Neal knew it was the delivery from the Japanese restaurant, he felt a spark in his stomach, as if Bart was back.

He paid for the sushi and sat back down. He opened the bag and saw that they'd forgotten to include chopsticks. Neal didn't like eating with his fingers when he was working. Was there anything worse than smearing condiments on your keyboard? Having to navigate sticky keys, the laptop heating up and smelling like nam pla? Neal went to the kitchen and got a fork and knife. He wasn't happy about it. Eating sushi with cutlery was depressing, deflating in an odd way, as if he was letting himself down.

He shoved a bite of California roll in his mouth and read the list of perks LeBlanc had negotiated when he was hired. The six-figure salary plus commission was standard for someone with his experience; the car and driver, the accounts at trendy restaurants, and the private tailor were perks that only the top executives received. They must've really wanted him, because they approved these perks—although oddly enough there was no record that LeBlanc had ever used them. Maybe he just wanted to see what he could get.

Neal did a quick scan of LeBlanc's browser history for the last twelve months. It was pretty boring reading. LeBlanc spent some time looking up political events around the world, but Neal decided that was because he was tracking currencies, and LeBlanc appeared to take an unusually high interest in the weather and agriculture reports. But a couple of deleted Google searches stood out—LeBlanc had looked for a book on maritime law. That seemed strange. Maybe it wasn't. Neal didn't have a clue and he really needed a clue. Anything.

He pulled up the phone records for LeBlanc's corporate account. There were several phone calls to and from the resort in the Dominican Republic, and calls to clients, restaurants, even a few colleagues. That was it. But this was LeBlanc's company phone. Most people used a personal line. Neal did. There are some things you don't want your employer to know about you. For example, if you want to send a picture of your erect penis to your boyfriend, you should probably do that on your personal device.

Neal also had asked the IT guys to pull up all the text messages from LeBlanc's company phone, including deleted ones. He looked at their report, and there was one slightly cryptic incoming message that had been deleted. It said simply, "Confirmed." It was from a number with a 345 country code. A quick cross-check on the internet and Neal learned it was from the Cayman Islands. He called the number and heard a recorded message. It was a bank called the CIBC Trust Company Limited. It could be nothing. Confirmation of a transaction he'd done for a client. LeBlanc had been meticulous, leaving no trace, but maybe someone on the other end had gotten sloppy. It was worth looking into.

If LeBlanc was hiding somewhere in the Caribbean, and everything seemed to point in that direction, then Neal was going to need someone who knew the region, someone who had contacts with the local authorities. He sent an email to an old friend who worked in the State Department. She'd know whom to call.

He closed the lid on his laptop and took a sip of his beer. He was tired, but not sleepy. He turned on his television and looked at his meager DVD collection. He couldn't decide between *L. A. Tool & Die* or *Kansas City Trucking Co.* They were classics and he'd watched them over and over since Bart left. Neal didn't like the new kind of porn, the Titans and twinks, but there was something about Joe Gage's workingman erotica that turned him on—probably because he didn't encounter that many workingmen. He chose the truck drivers. He drained his beer and let his pants drop to his ankles. It was time this fancy couch got some stains.

Bryan dropped the money off at the cottage he'd rented and then returned to the condo. He didn't park and enter the building; instead he sat in his rental car and watched the man in the yellow Jeep. He was still there, watching the condo. It was night and the rain had intensified. That made it easy for Bryan to go unnoticed, but also made it hard to see what was going on. The lights were still on in the apartment and the doors to the balcony were gaping open, swinging in the wind. It looked as though someone was home, someone who didn't care if the floor got wet. Bryan wasn't sure why he'd returned. He had made a substantial deposit into Cuffy Ebanks's bank account just in case something happened and he needed to cut and run. He could've stayed hidden, walked away from the condo as he'd planned. But the fact that someone was watching the apartment meant that someone knew about the money, and if so, someone would scour the island to find him. This was not good. Bryan needed time, a few days, maybe longer, to pull off his final move.

At around ten o'clock, Bryan saw a car pull up and park next to the Jeep. Leighton hopped out holding a newspaper over his head against the rain and climbed into the passenger side of the Jeep. Bryan sighed. You couldn't trust anybody these days.

Bryan remembered meeting Leighton at a forex confer-ence in Miami. He was ambitious, and his bank in the Cay-mans was actively pitching US brokers for clients who might want an offshore tax shelter. This was something that Brian didn't want to do for his clients. He thought they should pay taxes. Maybe it was because his dad had been a high school teacher, but there were too many rich people paying too little. Dodges and loopholes and deductions: it was a shell game. The rich stayed rich while the infrastructure and the public

school system collapsed. Who wanted to live in a society filled
with crumbling bridges and uneducated nitwits? But after a
few drinks, Leighton began to tell Bryan that he could fix certain things—residency status, visas, maybe even a passport—
and Brian began to take an interest. Leighton had delivered,
no doubt. He'd done everything he said he would and more.
Brian would've written him a glowing letter of recommenda-
tion. That's why it was so disappointing to see that he was
capable of betrayal. After a few minutes Leighton and the guy
in the yellow Jeep got out and walked across the street to the
condo. Bryan cracked his window open to get a clearer view
and watched as Leighton reached into his pocket and pulled
out a key. Both men were wearing latex gloves. Bryan assumed
it wasn't to keep their hands dry.

It took less than five minutes for them to figure out he
was gone. He watched the men exit the condo. The guy from
the Jeep wasn't happy. He was yelling and jabbing his finger
into Leighton's sternum. Bryan almost felt sorry for Leighton,
but hadn't he paid him enough? If he wanted a bigger cut he
should've said something. Bryan would have given him a bonus.
Of course he didn't feel that sorry for him; if Bryan *had* been
home, he would be dead right now and they'd be carting the
duffel bags out to their cars.

The guy gave Leighton a shove and then got back in his
Jeep and drove off. Leighton stood in the rain. Bryan couldn't
tell if he looked frustrated or forlorn, but he was obviously
giving the situation some thought. Eventually Leighton peeled
off his latex gloves, dropped them on the street, and got in
his car.

Bryan let Leighton drive off, then started his car and
followed.

He had never followed anyone before. He'd seen people do it in movies. He knew you weren't supposed to get close, just close enough to keep an eye on the vehicle without being seen. As it turned out, it wasn't difficult, even in the downpour, to keep Leighton's car in view.

A few minutes later Bryan saw Leighton pull into the drive of a modest bungalow. As he drove past he saw Leighton run from his car to the front door. Bryan kept driving until the bungalow was out of sight. He found a spot and pulled over to the side. What was his plan? Should he confront him? Offer to renegotiate? That seemed like the smartest move. He'd offer Leighton another million or two. It only seemed fair. He wouldn't have gotten this far without Leighton's help.

He turned off the engine. The car rental company had kindly left an umbrella in the backseat, and Bryan held it up over his head as he walked back along the road toward Leighton's bungalow. The only light was from his front porch and the dim glow from a few houses nearby. Leighton's house looked freshly painted, white with aquamarine shutters. Bryan could tell that he took pride in it. The garden was manicured and there was a path lined with conch shells leading to the veranda. Bryan stooped and picked one up, turning it upside down, draining the rainwater. They were substantial shells: bigger than his fist and twice as heavy. He didn't know what he was going to do with it exactly, but he figured he might have to defend himself. You couldn't be too careful. What if there was trouble? What if Leighton knew kung fu?

Bryan knocked on the front door and waited. He was nervous; he didn't know what to expect really, but he assumed that Leighton would be happy to have one or two million dollars dropped in his lap. Although the reverse could be just as true: Maybe Leighton wanted all the money. Maybe he was greedy.

As the rain pounded the umbrella, Bryan got a better idea. It wasn't an elaborate plan, but it might be effective. He'd still offer to give Leighton more money, but he'd start by smashing him in the head with the conch, then tying him up and having a chat. Play hardball first, then give in with cash. With the element of surprise and a good hard swing, it could work. Leighton seemed like a reasonable guy. Bryan was confident they could come to some kind of accommodation.

As Leighton opened the door, Bryan sprang forward and swung the conch as hard as he could, attempting to deliver an overhead smash to Leighton's skull. But the umbrella snagged in the doorway, impeding Bryan's lunge and causing him to stumble so that he missed the top of Leighton's head and instead plunged the spire of the conch straight into his left eye, knocking off his glasses, driving through the soft tissue and into his brain.

Leighton dropped dead on the floor, his limbs gently spasming, the shell protruding from his eye socket.

It was the gnarliest thing Bryan had ever seen.

Bryan dropped the umbrella at the door and stepped inside. He felt his bowels clench and lurch.

Had he just shit himself? Was he about to?

He leaned close to Leighton. "Hey. Hey, man. Can you hear me?"

Leighton was unresponsive.

Bryan gasped. The pressure from his bowels increased, a churning commanding him to shit. This was not what he'd had in mind, not at all, and yet it didn't take a genius to see that killing Leighton solved his problem.

Bryan had seen enough television to know that he had to wipe his fingerprints off the shell and hide the body somewhere. Ideally, he would take Leighton out to sea and sink him in deep water. Ideally, he would go into Leighton's bathroom and relieve himself. This was not an ideal moment for either option. What if Leighton had a wife? A partner? He had to get the body out of there as quickly as he could. Bryan clenched his sphincter and broke out in a cold sweat.

Careful not to touch anything else, he searched Leighton's pockets and found his car keys, then went outside and opened the trunk. The combination of dense foliage and a tropical downpour meant that he could probably pull this off without anyone seeing. He came back and picked Leighton up by the armpits and dragged his body out of the house. It was strange that Leighton's underarms were as clammy as his handshake. Maybe clammy people were not to be trusted.

Bryan gently dumped Leighton's body into the trunk, the trunk light glinting off the conch, a little spark of pink opalescence jutting grotesquely out of Leighton's face. He carefully wiped the conch with the end of Leighton's shirt and shut the trunk.

Bryan's bowels lurched again and he almost lost it, almost shit himself right then and there. But he clenched his teeth, tightened the muscles in his rectum, and scurried back to turn off the lights and shut the front door. That done, he picked up his umbrella, turned, and ran.

The rain continued to pound as Bryan slowed his jog to a quick shuffle. He didn't want any witnesses to say they saw someone running from the house. But he wasn't trying to flee a crime scene; his guts were on fire, his bowels screaming. Bryan realized he wasn't going to make it to his house; he wasn't even going to make it to his rental car. He couldn't hold it any longer. His bowels began moving whether he wanted them to or not. He ducked into the brush—ignoring the rain and the distant barking of a dog—and frantically dropped his pants. He squatted there, under the umbrella, and unleashed a violent torrent of shit.

Piet sipped his daiquiri and waited for the merengue to end. The merengue was not a sexy dance. He preferred the *bachata*. He could tell a lot about how a woman was in bed by the way she danced the *bachata*—the soft, rolling ass motion punctuated by the pop of the hips on the four—but the merengue told him nothing.

A few drops of condensation fell from his glass onto his lemon-yellow guayabera. Piet reached up to the bar for a paper napkin to blot them. He knew he looked crisp against the humidity, his chocolate-colored slacks freshly pressed, his leather shoes polished to perfection, and his hair sculpted by sweet-smelling gel.

The band segued to a salsa, again not as good as a *bachata*, but a decent enough indicator of sexual potential. As the dancers began to move, Piet scanned the crowd. He'd been trained by the police to read crowds for suspicious individuals and terrorists, and now he used the same skill to look for women.

The moon was full and gave a soft glow to the dancers as they moved to the beat. Piet had been on the floor a couple of times with young women—tourists who thought dancing with him was some kind of bucket list experience, a selfie to post on their social media—but like all serious playboys, he was happy to wait for something worth his time.

This wasn't the slickest club in Willemstad; in fact it wasn't a club, it was a bar on the beach that happened to have a good Latin band on Friday nights. The bartenders made a great daiquiri, though, and the joint was filled with bored tourists looking for something to do on their holiday in Curaçao.

Piet caught her out of the corner of his eye and turned to get a better look. She was pretty, but not beautiful, with long blond hair and a slash of red lipstick against skin that looked freshly sunburnt. He was a good judge of age and guessed she was in her late thirties. He liked women to be a certain age. Too young and they wouldn't know what they were doing, and honestly, what's the fun in that?

He watched her move to the salsa, her body undulating under a flowing beach dress, a belt made from looping silver circles draped across her hips. The dress was open at the neck, revealing a small gold crucifix nestled between her breasts. He could tell that she didn't really know how to dance the salsa: she wasn't following the prescribed moves, she was freely improvising, spinning and stepping to her own beat.

Piet smiled. Even though he was a former policeman, he didn't like people who followed the rules; it showed they lacked self-confidence. They might know all the steps and be able to perform without a mistake, but what they gained with precision they lost in passion. It was all about the ability to be yourself, to feel the music, to not care what anyone thought. That's what made someone a good lover—you had to be confident enough to let yourself get carried away.

A *bachata* started. Piet put his drink up on the bar and moved toward her.

They'd been dancing for almost an hour when he suggested they get a drink. He followed her back to her table, signaling a waitress for two daiquiris.

"You're a fantastic dancer."

She smiled and tucked a loose strand of hair behind her right ear. "You too."

Piet grinned. "I live for the *bachata*."

The cocktails arrived and they clinked their glasses together. Piet relaxed, sitting back in his chair and letting the breeze off the ocean cool his head. He tried to make small talk. "Are you here on vacation?"

She shook her head. "A friend's destination wedding." She took another sip of her drink. "Actually, not even a close friend. A coworker. I just thought it'd be fun to get away for a while."

"And are you having fun?"

She smiled. "Absolutely."

And then her face changed. She leaned close to him and said, "But the humidity is killing me and I desperately need a shower. Would you like to join me?"

"In a shower?"

She nodded.

Piet raised his glass to her. "I can scrub your back."

He followed her as she led the way, cocking his head slightly to the side for a better angle, studying the curve of her buttocks as she strode out of the bar and climbed into a taxi.

Piet had a unique relationship to women's bottoms. Not only was he a connoisseur of *culo*, an aficionado of ass, but he felt that women's asses communicated to him, through signs and semaphores. They sent him messages, gave him instructions, told him how they wanted to be caressed or if they preferred to be roughed up a bit. They teased, they invited, they told him stories of heartache and pain, triumph and ecstasy. His ability to read an ass wasn't a superpower; it was a skill he'd developed by paying close attention.

Her ass told him a story. It was a round but not spherical ass, slightly oversize but not wide; it was, he could tell, spectacular, the perfect combination of dance-floor firm and bedroom soft. But while her ass blushed at his unspoken appraisal, it told him to go gently, that it had been neglected and mistreated in the past, and it was lonely. The tourist's ass needed a friend more than anything else.

One of the few positives of having a genetic condition that gave him disproportionately short arms and legs was that the achondroplasia didn't affect his face, which was of normal size and handsome, or his genitals, which were quite large. Piet assumed that if he were six feet tall, like his father, he probably would've had a generous but normal-size penis. But he was only four-foot-seven, so when they finally got to her hotel room and he slipped out of his slacks, she looked at his erection and said, "Oh my."

What did a murderer eat for breakfast? Should he have what the menu called the "Pirate's Breakfast" or go with coconut French toast? "Dead men tell no tales," as the pirates say, but Bryan doubted that pirates really wanted to tuck into a pile of hash browns, pancakes, bacon, and eggs—although maybe that was the difference between a pirate and himself. He didn't swashbuckle a cutlass or fire a musket; he'd murdered a man with a decorative shell. A real pirate might have a robust appetite after a night spent pillaging, and it might make sense to carbo-load before enslaving the women and children and carting away the town's booty. That's hard work in the hot sun. But Bryan knew he wasn't really a pirate. He didn't want to be reminded of what he'd done, so he went with the coconut French toast and a second coffee.

The walls of the restaurant were painted in garish tropical greens and yellows, and there was a large mural of happy monkeys drinking Miller Lite. Arranged on the bar were a couple of large conch shells that gave him pause. He hadn't meant to kill Leighton. That was not the plan. He consoled himself with the knowledge that it was justifiable homicide; there were mitigating circumstances. He wasn't some kind of thrill-killer or psychopath. It was entirely accidental, and if he wasn't already in hiding for embezzling millions of dollars, Bryan might have even come clean to the police, told them it was all a joke gone wrong. No one in his right mind would drive a conch shell through someone's eye socket. Bryan LeBlanc wasn't a killer. But then, as he poured maple syrup on his coconut French toast, he realized that maybe Cuffy Ebanks was. Maybe you didn't fuck with Cuffy Ebanks, because you never knew what that dude would do.

The sound of the shower woke him up. Piet lay on the bed and felt around his mouth with his tongue. His upper lip was swollen slightly. He'd bitten his lip when she hopped off his cock, put her legs on either side of his head, and slammed her pelvis down on his face, violently thrusting her pussy against his mouth and moaning, "Eat me," until she came. Punched in the mouth by a wild pubis—Piet felt lucky he hadn't lost a tooth. Then again, if he had, it would've been worth it. His leg muscles were sore, and sometime in the night he'd managed to stub his toe by kicking the lamp off the nightstand. They'd had sex for hours and now he lay there exhausted, wounded, and famished.

Piet heard the distinct marimba sound of his cell phone ringing. The phone was sitting on the bedside table and he saw that the call was from a number in the 212 area code. New York, New York, USA. That was unusual. He didn't have any friends in the city. It could mean someone was calling with a job. Free-lance detective work was hit-or-miss, and he didn't want to let an opportunity pass him by, but when he reached for the phone, he heard the bathroom door open and let the call go to voice mail. Work could wait. He had his priorities.

The tourist came out of the bathroom, drying her hair with a towel, her admirable ass wrapped in a terry cloth bathrobe. She smiled. "I hope you like eggs. I ordered breakfast for us."

Piet grinned back. "I love eggs."

"Good. You're going to need your strength." She sat down on the bed and pulled the sheet back. Normally he might have felt self-conscious, his small body exposed like this, laid bare for an examination, but then she reached down and gave his penis a gentle squeeze. "Because I'm not through with this beast yet."

Neal plucked the menu out of the seat back in front of him and scanned the options. He turned to Seo-yun and said, "They have hummus."

"Hummus?"

"The chickpea dip."

Seo-yun blinked at him. "I know what hummus is."

"Don't get me wrong, I like hummus. I just think it's funny that you spend thousands of dollars to fly business class and the snack is hummus."

"I want to serve hummus at my wedding." She smiled. "Hummus and guacamole."

"Congratulations. When are you tying the knot?"

Seo-yun laughed. "Oh, I don't think I can go through with it. Feels like a trap."

Neal didn't know what to say, so he decided to say nothing. He didn't know Seo-yun, just knew her reputation at work, which was impeccable. It was rumored that she was somewhat Asperger-y. Of course the HR department was careful to couch any amateur diagnosis in its own unique legalese. There was concern expressed by one of her supervisors, who wrote, "While she excels at her job, she does not generate cultural synergy among the team." That was typical of HR. Give someone a compliment while expressing some obscure concern about something vague. Neal had no idea what "cultural synergy" meant. She seemed nice enough to him.

Other than that, there wasn't a lot of information about her. She wasn't on social media. There were no warnings in her personnel file. She was, by all accounts, an ideal employee.

Neal suspected that there might have been some friction between her and LeBlanc. The higher-ups gave LeBlanc credit for the department's successes, even though she was the managing director. Not that there was any evidence that LeBlanc had knowingly usurped her—that's just how Wall Street operated. The patriarchy, alive and well, grooming the young, dumb, and full of come to take the reins from the old, coddled, and in need of Viagra. It seemed strange that there were so many talented women not getting the credit they deserved, and yet 99 percent of the fraudsters, crooks, and hapless investors he went after were men. It was ironic. In a real way, a woman like Seo-yun had more of a grudge against the company than LeBlanc, and yet it was LeBlanc who'd been the embezzler.

The flight attendant leaned over them and asked if they wanted a beverage. *Why not say drink?* he thought. *Let's be adults here.* Seo-yun asked for bourbon, Neal a white wine.

Seo-yun turned in her seat to face him and said, "I've never been on an adventure."

"Never?"

She shook her head. "Usually I just go on a business trip. You know, a conference or something. This is way more exciting." She grinned. "A manhunt."

Neal laughed. "Usually I'm staking out a pizza place in Jersey, waiting for some poor schlub to pick up a pie so I can hit him with a court order."

She sighed. "I don't expect this will be that easy. Bryan's not playing by the rules. I kind of admire him for it."

"Even the smartest people make mistakes. We'll find him."

"You sound pretty sure of yourself."

Neal shrugged. "Well, even if we don't, we'll have an adventure."

The flight attendant served the drinks and Seo-yun raised her glass. "Here's to adventure."

Neal tapped his glass against hers. "Happy hunting."

She looked at him. "I'm unclear on one thing."

"What?"

"If we find him, then what do we do?"

"It's tricky. In any other situation I'd call in law enforcement, have them arrest him or seize his property with a court order." Neal took a sip of wine. "If we can't go to the police, I'm not sure what we can do. That's why we've got reinforcements meeting us in George Town."

"Reinforcements?"

"An ex-cop from Curaçao. A friend who works for the State Department said he was really good at this kind of thing."

"Like a mercenary?"

"A private detective."

Seo-yun smiled. "Some muscle."

Neal watched as she knocked back the rest of her whiskey. "Even with, like you said, muscle on our side, I'm not sure what we can do legally. If we convince LeBlanc to return the money, we won't be able to bring him back unless we offer him a deal."

"Or stuff him in our luggage."

Neal raised an eyebrow. She was signaling the flight attendant for another miniature bottle of bourbon. The attendant brought her two, and Neal watched her crack both bottles and dump them into her glass. She tucked a strand of hair behind her ear and took a slurp.

"We can't break the law. I want to be clear on that."

Seo-yun giggled as if the idea was funny. "I'm just here to provide tech support."

"There're a lot of variables. I'm not so sure he's in the Caymans."

"He's got to be there. All the other bank accounts are closed, but a couple of his transactions were routed through a Cayman account."

"The money may have gone through there, but that doesn't mean he's there. If I were him I wouldn't get anywhere near it. He could be anywhere."

Seo-yun shrugged. "He could convert it to cash."

"Really?"

"You'd need a bank manager to look the other way or be in on it. And you'd need a pickup truck."

Neal nodded. "Or a boat."

Seo-yun raised her glass. "Or a boat."

Lunch—a dour chicken breast stuffed with cheese—came and went, along with a couple of glasses of white wine for Neal and another bourbon for Seo-yun. She'd fallen asleep. Neal pulled a paperback out of his bag, *A Single Man* by Christopher Isherwood. Neal didn't know why he'd picked it up at the airport bookstore, but it had called out to him. Not that he was enjoying the read; the wine made it hard to concentrate and the book was making him feel sad. He didn't like the idea of hitting the ground in Grand Cayman like a morose drunk.

Neal wasn't sure what they were accomplishing except making the CEO feel they were doing something. He knew that if he were in LeBlanc's shoes, he would have moved the money into something easily transportable, maybe converted the cash into bonds and taken them to Argentina or Uruguay or even somewhere in Eastern Europe. The hope was that something had gone wrong. It didn't matter what it was, just something to throw a speed bump into his path and give them enough time to find him. What happened after that, well, Neal had no idea. He hoped the private detective would know what to do.

Neal had barely gotten twenty pages in when he felt a tap on his shoulder. He turned toward Seo-yun as she leaned close to him and said, "Can I ask you something personal?"

Neal recoiled a bit from the whiskey on her breath. "Sure."

"Are you a homosexual?"

"Yes."

"I thought so."

"It's that obvious?"

She gave him a funny look.

"I'm joking. I know it's obvious,"

She smiled and shifted in her seat, leaning closer. "So you like to suck cock?"

Neal raised an eyebrow. This wasn't a conversation he wanted to be having with a business colleague, but she seemed genuinely curious, so he decided to give her a genuine answer. "Among other things, yes."

Seo-yun grinned and clapped her hands together. "Me too." She gave him a playful punch in the shoulder. "We have something in common."

Piet didn't like missing person cases. They rarely ended with hugs and kisses. Half the time the people who disappeared were trying to escape something: an asshole spouse, controlling parents, a disgruntled loan shark, feelings of despair and helplessness. The other half of the time people were missing because something bad had happened to them. These cases typically involved the discovery of a corpse.

Piet studied the photo he'd been sent: a picture of a handsome enough Caucasian guy in a suit and tie who went by the name Bryan LeBlanc. The dude looked as if he had money. For sure Piet's client did. They'd wired a fat retainer into Piet's bank account in Willemstad and told him to spare no expense. The only lead they had was this resort in Punta Cana. It was the last place LeBlanc had been seen, and so Piet was on a plane, flying first class to the Dominican Republic.

The Playa Palms Resort was only a short cab ride from the airport, but Piet treated himself and rented a convertible.

He'd called ahead, spoken to the manager of the resort and the head of security. They confirmed that LeBlanc had been there. There was no record of any complaints by him or about him. LeBlanc had kept a low profile, paid his bill, and left. Piet was hoping he could talk to some of the waiters or bartenders and start to build a picture of this guy. The information he got from his client didn't tell him anything. All he knew was this missing person lived up to his name—the only thing everyone agreed on was that he was white.

The resort was one of those all-inclusive adults-only places that catered to honeymooners and couples trying to get away from their bratty children. Piet assumed there would be some single men and women staying there, people hoping to read a book on the beach, drink some rum, and maybe hook up with each other in the evening. But it wasn't a swingers club; this resort was classy, with tall open buildings made to look authentic by having palm fronds stuck into every conceivable nook and cranny and rattan wrapped around every piece of brightly cushioned furniture.

Piet checked in and then met with the head of security. She had very kindly arranged for the people who had met LeBlanc to stop by her office for a chat. It was slow going. Piet didn't speak Spanish—a drawback of growing up on one of the Dutch-speaking islands—and the employees' proficiency in English was spotty. Piet learned that LeBlanc was a good tipper, liked Presidente beer, and didn't throw his used towels on the floor. He had eaten dinner a couple of times with two women who were also staying there, but the housekeeper had not found any used condoms in the trash. Mainly it seemed that LeBlanc had been relentlessly polite. The only breakthrough was when the resort's driver told Piet that he had taken LeBlanc to the ferry terminal in Santo Domingo instead of the airport, so that LeBlanc could catch the boat to Puerto Rico.

Piet walked out on the beach and sat down on the sand. The beach was lovely. But were Dominican beaches better than beaches on Curaçao? Not really. The sand was softer. Piet wondered if Playa Palms had imported the sand. Resorts did that sometimes, bringing in truckloads of soft sand for the paying customers. He let out a sigh. He wanted to curl up on that nice imported sand and take a nap. First day on the case and he was already tired. This was the problem with police work: it was slow, methodical, and exhausting. His client would be expecting him to drive down to Santo Domingo and interview the ferry-boat workers, but Piet decided he'd sleep on it. He could drive there in the morning and see if anyone recognized LeBlanc. Maybe he hadn't gotten on the boat. Maybe he had. Piet would know more in the morning. Right now, he needed a drink.

Piet went to his room and changed into a fresh guayabera; he might as well enjoy the Caribbean buffet while he was here. And who knew? He might get lucky. It wouldn't be the first time.

The bar was busy with guests fueling up with predinner cocktails. He walked up to the bar and ordered a rum and Coke. A drunk American man—Piet could tell he was American from his accent and knew he was drunk from the blotchy gin blossoms on his face—turned from the bar and bumped into Piet.

The man reeled back, spilling some of his piña colada, and shouted, "Midget!"

From the reaction of the people around them, you'd think the man had just announced he had a bomb. The buzz and good vibe of the bar evaporated.

The man's face reddened. "This midget made me spill my drink."

The bartender handed Piet his drink. Piet turned to the drunk American and said, "I'll be happy to buy you a new cocktail."

Another drunk tourist shouted from a table across the room. "Little people, Don. Little people."

The drunk—apparently his name was Don—shouted back, "If I wanted to be politically correct, I'd go to California. I know a midget when I see one."

Piet squeezed the lime into his rum and Coke and took a big swallow.

The drunk American stood in front of Piet, swaying a bit from the booze, and adjusted his cap. "Did I offend you, little fella?"

Piet noticed that Don's cap had the outline of a bald eagle and said USA in bright red machine-embroidered letters. He took another sip of his drink and rattled the ice around in the glass. Piet looked up at the drunk and said, "Let's take the asshole test."

Don blinked. "What?"

"The asshole test. Do you want to take it?"

Don straightened, looming as tall as he could over Piet. "You talk funny. Where're you from?"

"The Netherlands."

Don looked toward his friends and laughed. "A midget from the Low Countries. Isn't that what they call ironic?"

"Irony implies the opposite of what you normally expect." Don did a slow blink. "They teach you that in tulip school?"

Piet smiled and finished his drink. "Take your hat, for example. You would think a hat that proclaims USA would be made in the USA, but I'll bet you it isn't."

Don whipped the cap off his head and looked at the label. His expression changed. "Vietnam. Goddamn it, the midget's right." Don threw the hat at the bartender in disgust. "All right, what's this asshole test? Is that where you come up behind me and smell my farts?" Don laughed at his own joke. "Get it? Because you're at the right height to sniff my butthole."

Piet laughed too. "Good one. But that's not the test. Here . . ."

Piet motioned for Don to lean closer. Don bent down to hear what Piet had to say, and that's when Piet smashed his glass against the bar, breaking the top half off, and punched Don in the face with the jagged edges. Don shrieked and dropped his piña colada. He slipped on the creamy coconut cocktail and fell on his ass as blood spewed out of his face. "Oh my God!"

Piet stepped forward and said, "You're in shock, I know. Nobody likes to learn that they're an asshole."

Then he turned and left the bar. Piet realized he had a long night ahead of him. He'd be driving to Santo Domingo after all.

Bryan had started the evening calmly enough, eating fish and chips and drinking a lager in a local bar, watching the evening news to see if there were any reports of a murder or the mysterious disappearance of a local bank manager. Bryan couldn't decide if he was relieved there was no news or if that just added to the suspense. He could feel the pressure build in his chest and then he felt his cheeks get wet. It was embarrassing. He went through several paper napkins trying to dry his eyes.

Bryan unfolded a copy of the *Cayman Compass*, the islands' "most trusted news source." A sixteen-year-old boy had been arrested for riding a stolen bike; six attorneys had been named Queen's Counsel, whatever that meant; the blood bank was looking for donations in preparation for hurricane season; and there was a renewed push for tax transparency—nothing about some poor fucker with a conch shell sticking out of his face.

That was worth drinking to.

Bryan wondered if Leighton had any family nearby; someone must be wondering where he was. The family would be sad when they found him, heartbroken and angry at the unfairness of it all. Maybe Leighton had a girlfriend or a boyfriend who loved him. What about that? When someone dies there's a ripple effect, loss and sadness that travel outward in all directions until the absence of that person encompasses the world. Would someone clean out Leighton's bungalow the way Bryan had cleaned out his father's apartment? Bryan hadn't thought about the apartment in Long Island City since he'd left New York, but now he realized that the rent would come due in a few weeks, and the landlord would send an eviction notice and eventually be forced to hire a locksmith to open the door to his father's place. There was no one to contact, no one to claim the contents, so everything would be thrown away. The last traces of a life—a life full of food and friends and poetry—would end up in a dumpster in Queens. The walls would be repainted, the refrigerator replaced, maybe there'd be an upgrade to the stove and toilet, and then a new person would move in and there would be nothing left of his father: no trace he was ever on this planet, only what Bryan could remember. And Bryan was almost gone; he would be Cuffy soon.

The Terminal Don Diego in Santo Domingo was a large hangar-like structure where boats came and went and you could catch a ferry to San Juan, Puerto Rico. Piet had spent the night in his car, parked across the street, waiting for the ferry to dock. That gave him plenty of time to go over the case. Not that he needed any time. LeBlanc had stayed at the resort. That's all he knew. That's what a $25,000 retainer got you: something you could've found out by placing a phone call.

Piet missed being on the police force. There was some dignity in scrounging around, following leads on an important case. There was job security too. He made a bit more money working for private clients, but it wasn't like there was a ton of work. He could go months without a job, and lately he'd been doing a lot of divorce work: following a husband who was supposed to be golfing but was instead sexing up someone other than his spouse. It was easy enough—you just needed a digital camera and a telephoto lens—but intruding on people's sex lives bothered him. Solving a crime, righting a wrong—that was one thing, but ruining people's lives because they were seeking pleasure seemed like a good way to get bad karma. Piet wondered if he'd ever been on the other side of the camera in a divorce case. Chances were pretty good he had.

Was this really how he wanted to spend the rest of his life, digging up other people's dirt? He decided that after this case was closed he'd look for a different job. Maybe work as a house detective for one of the cruise ship lines. The cruise ship idea had some appeal; there was easy access to a rotating stream of women looking for a good time.

Piet watched as cars drove off the ferry and into traffic. People were coming out of the terminal, meeting friends, hailing cabs, and getting on with their day. Piet finished his coffee and crumpled the cup, tossing it on the floor. One thing you had to say about Dominican coffee, it was better than what he drank on Curaçao.

The ferry was in dock for a couple of hours before it would turn around and head back to Puerto Rico. Piet managed to talk his way on board and have a quick conversation with the captain, surreptitiously slipping him an American hundred-dollar bill and getting permission to talk to the crew about an American man who'd gone missing.

Piet made the rounds, flashing a picture, trying to find crew members, struggling to communicate in his limited Spanish, but no one remembered seeing LeBlanc. Piet was beginning to think that LeBlanc hadn't taken the ferry after all, until a waitress in the snack bar remembered him.

She was an attractive young Dominican, with soft brown skin, large dark eyes, and an ass that woke Piet up. If he'd had time, if they were on a dance floor, he might be interested in more than her recollections about LeBlanc.

"What do you remember about him?"

She fluttered her eyelids and said, "He was *guapo*." And then she remembered, "And a good tipper."

"Do you remember what he ate?"

She smiled. "A *hamburguesa con queso*."

Piet made a point of writing that down in his notebook. Not that it mattered, but he wanted her to feel she was being helpful. He had all the information he needed. LeBlanc had taken the ferry to Puerto Rico, which meant Piet was headed to San Juan. Piet thanked her and slipped her some money, then went off to make a phone call.

But when Piet told his client that he was following LeBlanc's trail to Puerto Rico, he was told to abandon that plan and get to the Caymans as soon as possible.

A light drizzle was falling, not really rain, but enough that you might want an umbrella if you were going to be out in it for long. Seo-yun declined the umbrella. She let the rain fall on her face. Droplets dotted her glasses and refracted the light. Neal stood under an umbrella emblazoned with the Ritz-Carlton logo and watched her get wet.

"You want to get under here?"

She shook her head. "It feels good." Nothing in her day-to-day existence felt as good as this warm tropical precipitation; her job, her apartment, her clothes, her stupid fiancé—none of it compared to this sensation. Was it all those dry years of being in classrooms and offices, working toward whatever goal she'd been convinced she needed to achieve? Well, she'd achieved it all and it didn't feel nearly as good as this. Simple, sensual pleasure. That's what was missing. It made her wonder if something was wrong with her, like some kind of neurological problem or vitamin deficiency that hadn't, until this moment, allowed her to take pleasure in simple things. What if she'd been dehydrated for decades? She made a vow to drink lots of water and take a dip in the hotel pool. She was going to be a sponge and absorb as much tropical moisture as she could.

Atlantic Starr began crooning from her cell phone. She sent the call to voice mail. Whatever her fiancé needed, well, he'd just have to wait.

"We should get inside."

She closed her eyes and felt the drizzle splatter her face.

"C'mon." Neal gently took her arm and led her through the glass door into the air-conditioned lobby of the First-Caribbean International Bank. Seo-yun shivered in the cold air. They'd called ahead and made an appointment with one of the private banking managers.

She had been expecting to be taken into an office, offered a cup of tea or a glass of water, and reassured by the manager that he would help in any way he could. But that's not what happened. Instead a young woman appeared and told them that the manager handling the account hadn't showed up for work. She didn't know where he was. She hadn't been involved in managing the account and there wasn't much she could tell them; there was no name on it, just an account number and they already knew that. She reminded them that the bank was a signatory to the US Patriot Act and all suspicious transactions would have been reported. She handed them the account manager's business card. That way they could call him directly.

"He should be in tomorrow," she concluded.

Seo-yun felt a shiver run through her body, and her skin dimpled with goose bumps.

Neal looked at the card and turned to Seo-yun: "Let's go find Leighton Stewart." Neal hooked his arm in hers and led her out of the building and back into the rain. "I'm sure they'll have a phone book at the library."

He popped the umbrella open as they crossed a little plaza called Heroes Square, although who the heroes were was unclear, and headed into the George Town library.

Seo-yun had overheard some tourists talking about the library, how it had some kind of historical importance on the island, but from the outside, it just looked like a municipal building that could've been in Fort Lee or Syracuse. But as they entered she noticed that the library was divided into two buildings. On one side was a large and well-appointed modern building that housed the actual working library, and on the other was a funky older building.

Seo-yun let Neal do the detective work. Not that it was going to require a skill any more refined than looking up Leighton Stewart's address and phone number in the phone book. But he was the investigator, so while he did that, Seo-yun walked into the old part of the library to see what was so special. The room itself was nothing unusual: a white room with windows and some empty shelves along the walls. There were no books, no tables, no card catalog. But when she looked up, she understood. The roof had been built by a shipbuilder who, perhaps incapable of constructing a standard roof, made a hull of a ship instead, so it looked as if an old Spanish galleon had fallen upside down on top of the room. It was insane. It was magic.

Seo-yun stood there and admired the woodwork. Here was proof that you could think differently, flip the script, and play to your strengths. Turn everything upside down. It was such a simple idea, and it was brilliant. As she looked at the roof she realized that she could not think of a single reason not to turn her world on its head. She wanted to live a life where tropical moisture had priority over making a lot of money.

Neal walked up alongside her. "Got it." He stopped and looked up at the ceiling. "Upside-down boat," he said.

She nodded. "He played to his strengths."

Her cell phone began to croon. Her fiancé was texting. He needed to know if she really wanted a soju cocktail at the reception. Everyone was waiting for her answer.

Piet sat in the lobby of the Ritz-Carlton Grand Cayman drinking a cup of coffee. He watched tourists walk by: pale and friendly, probably Canadian. A woman dressed in expensive resort wear complained to the concierge about the weather. She had that confident, entitled, thoroughly obnoxious attitude that people from the industrialized world liked to project on people in the Caribbean. The concierge assured her the rain would lift. Piet heard her say, "My husband came here to play golf," which made Piet chuckle. You could golf in the rain. The hotel would probably provide someone to hold an umbrella over her husband while he played. It was that kind of place.

Piet had seen the inside of some swanky hotels, but he had never checked in at one under his own name. He could get used to the luxury, he could see that, and maybe if this case lasted long enough he could pay for it himself. He was charging his client quadruple his usual rate because he was off Curaçao, on unfamiliar territory, and, well, why not charge them as much as he could? They were a big Wall Street firm; they practically minted money.

He had gotten a text from Neal Nathanson, the firm's representative, saying they were visiting the local bank and they should meet him at the hotel for lunch to figure out a plan, but that was two hours ago. Piet thought he should have heard from them by now. That, and he was getting hungry.

"Piet Room."

Piet turned and saw an affable-looking man standing next to him.

"Detective Grover." Piet stood and the two men shook hands. Piet pointed to a seat. "Thanks for coming on short notice. I don't have a lot of time."

The detective chuckled. "When Piet Room calls, I move mountains."

Piet couldn't help but notice that Grover had aged. His close-cropped hair was sparked with gray, and he was heavier, his paunchy gut protruding above his belt like a scoop of ice cream about to fall off the cone.

Grover settled into the chair and looked around. "You can't be staying here on your own dime."

Piet smiled. "Client is picking up the tab. You want a coffee?"

Grover nodded. "Have them throw a little Irish in it."

Piet signaled to the waiter.

"So why are you here? Another husband think his wife is cheating?"

Piet laughed. "I'm sure she is, but that's not why I'm here." He leaned forward. "It's a missing person case."

"You suspect something foul?"

Piet shrugged. "They won't tell me much. Good news is they're sparing no expense."

"Apparently."

"And they don't want the police involved."

"Because if we find the guy first, he might tell us something they don't want us to know."

"It's a Wall Street thing."

The coffee arrived and Grover licked the whipped cream off the top before taking a sip. "And so you called up your old pal because . . ."

"Just thinking I might need some backup. I don't know what I'm getting into."

"You know the laws here. I don't carry. Nobody carries. We don't do firearms here, somebody could get hurt."

"What about nonlethal?"

"I might be able to dig up an old Taser." Grover chuckled. "But then you have to come for dinner. You know Mary makes a great grouper escabeche."

Piet nodded at Grover's gut. "I can see."

The Harbor House Marina was the largest boat dealer on Grand Cayman, and although Bryan would have liked to buy a boat from a private citizen in a discreet cash deal, there just weren't as many available as he thought there would be, and none that served his purpose. But he wasn't worried. If he had to buy a panga boat and motor all the way to the Bahamas to buy a proper sailboat, he would.

Bryan pulled his rental car into the lot and parked next to a large industrial-looking building with a clump of palm trees plopped in front. He'd used the phone in the rental house to call ahead and had spoken to a chirpy saleswoman. She said they might have what he was looking for, and so here he was, ready to shop, half a million dollars in cash burning a hole in the trunk of his car.

The salesperson's name was Teresa, and she was one of those sun-kissed and athletic women who were into outdoorsy activities like rock climbing and parasailing. "This," she said, "could be your lucky day."

Bryan followed her out toward the marina. He tried to keep his eyes from wandering over her body, which was attractively packaged in white jeans and a pink polo shirt. Sex was a distraction and now was not the time. He had to stay focused. Once he was off the island he could think about all those complicated things that normal people take Xanax to avoid thinking about.

They walked past a large powerboat hanging in the air, attached to a gigantic contraption, a skeletal cube on wheels, designed to lift boats in and out of the water. He stopped and stared.

"You sure you want a sailboat?"

He turned to Teresa and smiled. "What can I say? I'm a romantic. I like the wind."

She led him to the end of the marina, past several boats: mostly powerboats used for day fishing and a few smaller sailboats. There, gleaming in the water, was an almost new Beneteau Oceanis 38.1. Bryan had seen pictures of the Oceanis line of sailboats. They had a sleek, ultramodern design that sailors either loved or hated. Bryan hadn't been a fan, but now, seeing it in person, he was impressed. It was beautiful.

Teresa climbed aboard. "A couple from Miami bought it and had it shipped here, then he caught her in bed with the nanny."

"So they're getting divorced."

She nodded and Bryan could detect a glint in her eye.

"You're not telling me the whole story."

"Seems the husband wasn't mad. Took off his clothes and got in bed with them both, and the wife decided that was too much."

"Boundaries are important."

She held out a hand to help Bryan get on the boat. He didn't need her assistance, but he wanted to touch her, so he let her help him.

"It's in the cruiser configuration. Thirty-eight-footer. Two cabins. Head. Separate shower. It's basically outfitted for long-term use. You could live full-time on it, if you wanted."

"How's it for storage?"

She shrugged. "Typical. But it's got two cabins and you could provision the smaller one for long hauls."

Bryan had hoped for a forty-two-footer or larger, but this one was ready to go and he was used to sailing boats about this size. He could get off the island in a day or two.

Teresa crossed her arms and looked at him. "What're you thinking?"

"I was hoping for something bigger."

"Story of my life."

He raised an eyebrow. Was she flirting?

She coughed. "Sorry. Joke."

He smiled. "How much do they want for it?"

"Do you want to take it out for a test run?"

"She looks pretty solid."

"It's a great boat." They looked at each other for a moment and then she said, "Two twenty-five."

Bryan tried to appear thoughtful. He ran his fingers through his hair as if he was struggling to come to a decision. "How soon could you get her seaworthy for me? Turn one of the cabins into storage? Make sure all the ropes are good?"

"Might take a couple of days, but we'll make it happen."

"I'd like to keep this purchase discreet."

"Naturally."

He figured she might be used to selling boats to drug smugglers and rich people trying to invest in tax dodge schemes. "Do you take cash?"

Teresa brightened. "Mr. Ebanks, we'll take payment in any form you like."

Bryan shook her hand. "Call me Cuffy."

The hostess led Neal and Seo-yun across the patio toward a table where Piet sat eating a cheeseburger.

Seo-yun turned to Neal and said, "This is the muscle?"

Neal shrugged. "I've never worked with him before, but he comes highly recommended."

Piet wiped his hand on his napkin and extended it. "You must be Mr. Nathanson."

Neal shook his hand. "Call me Neal. This is my colleague Seo-yun Kim."

Piet took Seo-yun's hand and their eyes locked. It was only for a second, but Neal noticed a brief spark of something pass between them. Neal remembered when he met Bart and they'd shared a look like that from across a crowded room. A few months later Neal was buying the most expensive couch he'd ever seen.

Seo-yun asked Piet, "What are you eating?"

"They call it a Caribbean burger but it's pretty much a normal burger."

"What makes it Caribbean?"

"Pepper jelly." Piet waved his hand at the empty chairs. "Sit. You should eat something. It's going to be a long day."

Seo-yun sat next to Piet and said, "Sure, I'll try a Caribbean burger." And then she took a french fry off his plate, dipped it in what looked like mayonnaise, and popped it into her mouth. Neal saw Piet smile, watching her lips as she chewed before taking a bite out of his Caribbean burger and sending pepper jelly spurting out.

The waiter came over and offered a menu, but Neal just said, "I guess we'll all have a Caribbean burger."

Piet wiped his lips. "You won't be sorry."

Neal did feel a bit of remorse about eating the Caribbean burger. Pretty much every time the car hit a bump he got a repeater burp of beef grease and sweet hot pepper in the back of his throat. He really wished he'd gone up to his room and brushed his teeth before they left, but maybe he could use the strange belchy feeling to his advantage, get in the bank manager's face, get to the bottom of this.

Neal had found Leighton Stewart's address in the George Town phone book; he just hoped the bank manager would be home. They pulled up in front of an adorable little bungalow, freshly painted white with aquamarine trim and with a cute walkway lined with giant conch shells.

They got out of the car, and Neal watched Piet stare at Seo-yun's ass. Of course her ass was right in his sight line, but it seemed to Neal that Piet was unnaturally fixated on it. He wished someone would look at his ass like that.

He followed Piet and Seo-yun up the crushed stone path toward the front door. All of a sudden Piet stopped and turned to them. "Let's get out of here."

Neal was confused. "Why? We just got here."

Piet sniffed the air. "You can't smell that?"

Neal caught a whiff of something sweet and trashy, like ice cream and rotting produce.

Seo-yun looked at Piet. "It smells like garbage."

Piet shook his head. "If you don't want the police involved in this case, we walk away right now."

Neal started to argue, but Piet cut him off.

"That's the smell of a corpse. We need to go."

They got back in the car as quickly as they could without looking suspicious. Neal didn't know what to think. It did smell funky but . . . a corpse? That seemed like a stretch. And if it was a corpse, did that mean LeBlanc had killed his accomplice? Or maybe it was LeBlanc's body. Neal heard Piet on his cell phone talking to someone in the police force. Apparently Piet had friends there who would treat the information as an anonymous tip.

Neal and Seo-yun exchanged a look, but Neal wasn't sure what the look was. Did she believe there was a corpse in the house? Or did she think Piet was bullshitting? But why would he be? It annoyed Neal. What had started out as a simple and logical search of a small island had suddenly become complicated.

He decided to take charge. "We should look at car and truck sales, new registrations, boat sales."

"That sounds like a good place to start," Seo-yun agreed.

Piet raised an eyebrow. "Why do you think he's buying some kind of transport?"

Seo-yun said, "He might need to get around the island. Move some stuff."

Piet nodded. "Okay, but he came here for a reason, right?"

"We think he came to see Leighton Stewart."

"Why?"

"That's what we're hoping to find out."

"Seems vague." Piet sucked his teeth, apparently thinking about something, and then turned to Neal. "Were you military?"

"I never served."

"Thought you might've been air force, Cyber Command or something."

"That sounds cool, but no."

"Police? You work in law enforcement?"

Neal shook his head. "Nope. And I'm not a lawyer or a licensed private investigator, if that's where you're going next."

"Diplomatic security?"

"No." Neal had never really had his credentials questioned before. It was irritating.

"I didn't mean to upset you," Piet said apologetically.

"I'm not upset."

Seo-yun interjected. "I'm sure you're good at your job, but I can assure you that Neal is also very good at his job."

Piet sucked on his teeth again and nodded. "You're the boss. I'll go to the Department of Vehicle and Drivers' Licensing and see if there are any new transactions. If he bought something, new or used, they'll have a record of it."

Seo-yun looked at Piet. "I'll come with you."

Neal raised an eyebrow at Seo-yun, then shrugged and said, "I guess I'll go talk to some boat dealers."

Grover had told Piet to wait for him at the police station, so Piet sat on a bench and watched Seo-yun stroll down the hallway. She walked past the Royal Cayman Islands Police Service crest: an English lion above three green stars. Underneath the crest was the official police motto: "We Care, We Listen, and We Act." A claim that Piet could arguably debunk based on past experiences working with the RCIPS. As far as he could tell they sometimes cared, never listened, and did whatever the hell they felt like doing. Grover was the exception to that. He could be discreet. Especially if there was some angle he could work later to his benefit.

Piet watched as Seo-yun did a pirouette and walked back toward him. She was on the phone. Apparently she had a lot going on, because her phone rang every fifteen minutes, sometimes more. And that's not counting the text messages. She paced back and forth, her head flopped to one side, as if the conversation she was having was the most boring thing in the world.

He could feel the sexual magnetism between himself and Seo-yun. Something about the way she ate the french fry off his plate was a signal. You didn't have to be a biologist to see that.

She spun on her toes, turned, and walked away from him. He thought, *Her ass is incredible.* Unlike the twitch and sling of other asses, hers spoke to him like no other ass he'd ever communicated with. He could hear Seo-yun's ass talking to him in his head:

I want to feel the sun on my skin. I want the wind to whip between my cheeks and cool my hot pussy. I want you . . .

She had a telepathic ass.

Piet focused his mind's eye and sent her ass a mental message. He would take her outside. He would do whatever she wanted. He could feel his penis stiffening in his pants.

"You look like you're trying to take a shit."

Piet looked up and saw Grover standing in front of him. He stood up. The front of his pants tenting awkwardly. Piet pulled his guayabera down to cover it. "Just thinking."

Grover laughed. "You want my advice, don't think so hard."

Piet changed the subject. "What did you find?"

"You're going to have to tell me about this case you're working on." Grover flipped his iPhone around and showed Piet a photo he'd snapped. "This ain't no selfie."

Piet put his fingers on the glass and zoomed in. The photo revealed a partly decomposing man with a giant conch shell sticking out of his face.

"What the fuck?"

Seo-yun came up behind him and looked over his shoulder at the photo. He was surprised that she didn't react. She just said, "That's not him." And then she went back to her call.

"Who is it?"

Grover cleared his throat. "Leighton Stewart. In his car. Parked in his driveway."

Piet nodded. "So . . . suicide."

Grover grunted. "Don't get cute with me. I want to know who you're looking for because I think he might know something about this."

"We were looking for him. Leighton Stewart."

"Then I guess I want to know why you're looking for him."

Piet spoke quietly. "They haven't told me. We're also looking for an American male. Thirtyish. Six feet tall. Average build, average weight."

Grover grimaced. "I got three thousand of those coming off a cruise line this afternoon."

"Apparently he needs a truck or a boat." Piet cleared his throat. "That's really all I know."

Grover did not look happy. "Maybe I'll take her in for questioning."

Piet shook his head. "They'll just hire a bunch of lawyers. You won't get anything."

"Can you at least give me a name?"

Piet saw Seo-yun hang up and put her phone in her purse. He moved close to Grover. "Bryan LeBlanc."

"I'll run the name and have my people check the car rentals and immigration, see if anything comes up. He had to enter the country at some point."

"Thanks."

"You can thank me when you come to the house for some grouper." With that, Grover grunted a good-bye and walked off down the hall.

Seo-yun walked toward Piet. He heard her ass speak again, a soft whisper inside his head: *Let's get it on.*

As he cruised down the Esterley Tibbetts Highway, Neal began to question his instincts. He'd already been to the Barcadere Marina, the George Town Yacht Club, and the Cayman Islands Sailing Club. He'd spent half the afternoon driving around and gotten nowhere. The George Town Yacht Club turned out to be a restaurant. Nobody knew anything about a boat bought or sold in the past few weeks. Not unless you counted a Jet Ski.

Neal had flashed a photograph of LeBlanc—the picture from his corporate ID card—but he just got shrugs and blank expressions. Everyone had seen someone who looked like that. The island was crawling with American tourists, and LeBlanc was just another good-looking Caucasian with money.

It was frustrating. How could someone just vanish? In a typical case he would have seized the assets by now and been done with it. The Caymans, the bank transactions, the weekend sailing lessons—it was too much of a coincidence not to be connected, and yet it wasn't adding up. The only promising news was a phone call from Piet to tell him that the smell at Leighton Stewart's bungalow was, in fact, Leighton Stewart's dead body. But while that was a clue, it didn't reassure him. Murder didn't fit with what he knew about LeBlanc. It didn't make sense. But then maybe the whole thing had gone sour and they'd be finding LeBlanc's body next.

Or he could be completely wrong. He didn't know. He didn't feel sure of anything.

Maybe the breakup with Bart had thrown his intuition off. He spent a good portion of every day brooding about their relationship and what he could've done or should've done or would've done if he'd just known how tenuous everything was. He could have rooted for the Mets. Would that have killed him? Bart thought tattoos were superhot. Why didn't he get one? Neal didn't have anything against tattoos. Bart had a few and was especially proud of his tattoo of Mr. Met as drawn in the style of Tom of Finland. It was, Neal had to admit, unlike any tattoo he'd ever seen before, the Mets' mascot, with his baseball for a head and his goofy grin, suddenly shirtless, revealing a muscular body, and sporting a massive erection practically leaping out of his baseball chaps. Sexualizing sports team mascots was original. And if you were going to put something permanent on your body, you probably wanted something original. What sports team mascot would Neal put on his biceps? You can't sexualize a Seahawk. He'd bought the couch for Bart, it was true, but maybe a couch just wasn't enough to base a long-term relationship on.

Neal pulled into the Harbor House Marina and parked, but he didn't get out of the car. Instead he let the seat fall back as far as it could and lay there, thinking. He realized his heart wasn't in it—he didn't feel like talking to anyone. He didn't want to canvass the employees and ask roundabout questions before showing the grainy photo of LeBlanc. He didn't want to see them shrug and hear them mutter apologies that they couldn't help him. It was all too dispiriting.

He got out of the car and took a stroll through the marina, past fishing boats and power cruisers. A few boats were pulling into slips, returning home with their cargo of sportfishermen and -women standing on the deck drinking beer and holding up bloody mahimahi. They were sunburnt and smiling, taking selfies with the dead animals. Neal didn't get it, but maybe that's what people did on vacation: they killed things and took pictures.

Not that he would know. He hadn't had a vacation in years. Why hadn't he taken Bart to Hawaii or the Bahamas or even Fire Island? Stuck his feet in the sand, drunk rum until he fell asleep, woken up, and killed something. Taken some pictures; made some memories.

Neal was ready to go back to the hotel and see how many mojitos he could drink when he came to a few sailboats. Some were tied in their berths and unoccupied. They were big enough to live on, like nautical RVs.

Nothing was happening on any of the boats except the sleek boat at the end. Workmen were busy restringing lines and hauling supplies aboard, seemingly prepping the boat for something, all of this activity overseen by a young woman in a pastel polo shirt.

Neal was good at finding people and recovering assets because he was logical and methodical. He didn't believe in hunches or Ouija boards or letting the universe guide him. But even so, there was usually a moment when the logic and the method lined up and he knew he was close to the truth. He remembered an old quote from a Sherlock Holmes mystery, where the coke-addled detective said: "When you have eliminated the impossible, whatever remains, however *improbable*, must be the truth." Seeing the boat, Neal felt something, and it wasn't the Caribbean burger and it wasn't his heartbreak. Neal would've bet his expensive couch that this was LeBlanc's boat.

Neal watched, trying to look casual. He waited until the woman stepped off the boat, and then he approached her. "Beautiful boat."

She nodded. "Yeah. She's a special one."

"Are you getting ready to put it on the market?"

She smiled at him. "Just sold it. But if you're looking, I can take your information."

Neal smiled back. "Do you have a card?"

She pulled a business card out of her pocket and handed it to him. "Just let me know what you're in the market for."

He watched her walk away and then pulled out his cell phone.

Seo-yun crouched in the backseat of the car on all fours. Her skirt had been lifted up against her back and her panties were looped around her left ankle. Piet was behind her, his pants around his ankles, his hands gripping her hips, his pelvis slamming away at her.

She'd never had sex outdoors before. But the sexual tension in the car had been too much to bear, so she'd suggested they just pull over. He'd found a kind of jungled-up cul-de-sac, so they kicked off their shoes and climbed into the backseat.

They left the car doors open so she could feel the sunlight on her face, the tropical air from the ocean caressing her skin. It was all so pleasant, like a really lovely picnic. The simple things. That's what she'd been missing. She slipped her hand under her bra and pinched her nipple. It made her come.

Of course she'd known they would end up somewhere like this. She saw how he looked at her in the police station. It was like a flashing neon sign that blinked the words FUCK ME in hot pink. She thought they might wait until night, maybe have a few drinks, end up in one of their hotel rooms; but when her fiancé called her for the fourth time in a half hour, well, she just turned to Piet and said let's get it on. Not that she said those words exactly. She was more direct. Now he was back there, groaning and saying something to her ass, having a conversation with it. Men, she decided, were strange.

Piet thrust hard, his cock going deep inside her, and she let out a little moan. It did feel good, she could admit that, and getting fucked alfresco was fantastic. It really was a shame she hadn't tried it sooner. Maybe that's why people moved out to the suburbs. It's easier to fuck outside if you have a backyard.

She heard her phone ringing inside her purse and reached into the front seat for it. Piet slowed his motion. "What're you doing?"

Seo-yun looked at the caller ID and said, "It's Neal." She answered the phone. "Hey, Neal." Piet had stopped thrusting. She turned her head and made a rolling motion with her fingers. "Keep going."

Piet began thrusting again, and she pushed the button for speaker and heard Neal ask, "What's happening?"

"We're just finishing up."

"Finishing up what?"

She looked back at Piet's face. His jaw was slack and his eyes were rolling up in his head. "He's coming."

Piet let out a low, guttural moan. She felt his cock spasm inside her and his body shudder.

"What?"

Seo-yun turned back to the phone. "I already came. So, you know, he's doing his thing."

She felt Piet's cock go soft and he stepped back, out of the car, and began pulling up his pants. Neal wasn't saying anything on the other end of the phone, so Seo-yun broke the silence.

"You'd like him. He's got a big dick."

Pearson Kilpatrick sat on a low wall and watched the American talk on his mobile. It was a nice scene: the marina in the foreground, the boats bobbing on dark water, and then the soft blue-green of the sea beyond, the kind of aquamarine that had an inner glow; you could only get that color by using oils. Acrylics just didn't let the light in.

The American seemed annoyed. By what, Pearson had no idea, but he'd been following him ever since he and the midget and the Asian woman left Leighton's house in a hurry. Pearson knew that the American and his friends were looking for the same thing he was looking for, the thing that he and Leighton had come close to stealing.

Leighton was his cousin. They'd grown up together. Gone to school. Got into mischief. All the things that boys do. Their parents worked at hotels and resorts on the island, which meant that they had gotten a taste of what it would be like to be rich like the tourists. Pearson wasn't impressed. Just because you acted better than everyone didn't mean you were. But Leighton wanted to be wealthy like the bankers and the celebrities who stayed at the resorts and bought mansions on the island, people like Taylor Swift, Dwayne "the Rock" Johnson, and billionaire Ken Dart. Leighton went to college, studied hard, and when he learned that almost $21 trillion in offshore funds was processed through Cayman banks, well, he studied harder. Got his foot in the door at a bank and worked his way up.

Pearson took a more relaxed, almost Rastafarian view of day-to-day living. Of course that changed, and the dreads came off, when he started taking his art seriously. But just because he was committed to being an artist didn't mean there was a demand for his work in George Town. The three or four galleries on the island specialized in art for tourists. Paintings of sea turtles and sandy beaches were fine, but they were not the kind of art he wanted to paint.

When Leighton showed up at his studio with the plan, it seemed simple and straightforward. Leighton pulled a couple of cold Mango Tango beers out of a paper bag and cracked them open. He handed one to Pearson and then sat at the table and laid it out.

"He'll have a new identity. So even if his body washes up, he's nobody anyone knows."

"Why do we have to kill him? Why not just take the money?"

"Because he'll find us and try to get the money back." Leighton sipped his beer. "He knows who I am. He's a criminal. He could kill us."

"You sure the money is there."

"I put it there."

"How much?"

"About fifteen million."

"And I get half?"

Leighton nodded.

Pearson wiped the sweat off his face. "We got no other choice?"

Leighton shrugged. "I don't know how else to do it."

"I'm not a murderer."

"Me neither."

The two cousins studied each other. Finally Pearson said, "It could look like an accident. He could drown."

Leighton shook his head. "We jump him in the condo. That's the easiest. If we have to put him on a boat, someone could see."

"Might be worth the risk."

Leighton brightened. "He could hang himself."

By the time they opened their third beer, they'd decided that a kind of assisted suicide was preferable to beating his brains in with a pipe. It would be hard to live with something like that.

Of course, when they got to the apartment he was gone. The money was gone. Their dreams of wealth snuffed out.

And then Leighton disappeared.

It had been three days now and there was no sign of him. Leighton wasn't the kind of guy to just up and leave his cushy job at the bank, but he hadn't come home or answered his phone or shown up for work—trouble done blow shell— and now Pearson was on his own. Either Leighton got the money and bounced off-island, cutting him out of the deal, or the guy really was a criminal and had done something to Leighton. Unless there was someone else involved, like this American guy and his friends.

He'd followed the American because he looked like he was in charge. In charge of what, Pearson didn't know, because none of them looked like the police; no way they were FBI; maybe they were CIA. If movies were any indication, the CIA was filled with weirdos.

Pearson didn't know if the American was looking for the guy or Leighton or the money, but he was going to get that money if it killed him. And then he was going to France.

What artist doesn't dream of France? With the loot he could set himself up in the City of Light—rent a studio in some funky suburb like Ivry-sur-Seine—and do the kind of painting that he'd always wanted to do. He could quit churning out paintings of Caribbean women with baskets of fruit on their head. He could stop slapping bright island color on crude landscapes of simple huts and flatly rendered palm trees. That work was crap. It was a waste of his talent. Even his boss at the gallery said so. His dream was to follow in the footsteps of painters like Eric Fischl, R. B. Kitaj, and Francesco Clemente. He was a serious artist, and the islands were holding him back.

Pearson Kilpatrick could draw. He could paint. Not only could he pronounce *chiaroscuro* correctly, he could do it too.

Pearson never thought he'd be involved in murder, but if art was about sacrifice, wasn't it better to sacrifice someone else?

He watched the American put his mobile in his pocket and walk back to his car.

Neal sat at the table eating a Caribbean Caesar salad that reminded him of a Cajun Caesar salad he'd had once in New Orleans and a chili ranch Caesar salad he'd had in Dallas and a Cabo Wabo Caesar supreme he'd had in Mexico. Throw some spicy grilled shrimp on lettuce, make up a name. It wasn't the most exciting thing on the menu, but maybe now that they were close to LeBlanc, he didn't have a big appetite for cheeseburgers with pepper jelly.

Neal saw Seo-yun walk into the lobby of the Ritz-Carlton. Piet was still outside; he seemed to be sending a text. Seo-yun smiled when she saw Neal and said, "Hey there." She pulled out a chair and joined him.

Neal leaned forward and spoke softly. "Can we talk?"

"Of course. What?" Neal hesitated. Seo-yun cocked her head. "Why are you being so weird?"

"It's none of my business but, you know, you're not supposed to fraternize with the subcontractors."

"Fraternize?"

Neal looked down at his salad. "You know what it means."

"You mean fucking him on the street?"

Neal's mouth dropped open. "You didn't."

Seo-yun laughed at him. "Is this an HR problem? Are you going to write me up?"

"Of course not."

"So what are you worried about?"

Neal softened. "I'm sorry. He makes me feel tense."

She smiled. "Maybe you're just jealous."

Something about the way she said it hit home, reminding Neal that he was lonely, that he wanted to desire and be desired as much as anyone. "Maybe I am."

"We can have a three-way later. Right now I'm famished."

Neal couldn't help it; he blushed. "Now that's an HR nightmare."

Seo-yun scanned the menu. "These manhunts really work up an appetite." She looked up at Neal. "That didn't come out exactly right."

Piet entered the restaurant and sat down at the table. When the waiter brought him a menu, he declined it with a shake of his head.

"You're not eating?" Neal asked, and took another bite of his salad.

"I'm having dinner with a friend."

Seo-yun looked at Piet. He shrugged. "Grover? You met him at the station this afternoon."

"You don't have to explain. I'm not the jealous type." She turned to Neal. "If the money's on that boat, we've got a lot of work to do."

Piet's eyebrow shot up. "Money? I thought we were looking for a person."

Neal swallowed, washing the shrimp down with some iced tea, and couldn't hide the irritation in his voice when he said, "We are."

Piet stared at Neal, then at Seo-yun. "It helps me if I know what I'm investigating."

"We're looking for a person who has some money," Seo-yun explained.

"But we're concentrating on finding the person," Neal clarified. "He may not have any money. He may have hidden it somewhere."

Piet glared at them. "Fine. You don't want to tell me everything, that's your deal. But that's why you think he's bought a boat. The big thing he has to move is money."

Seo-yun raised her shoulders. "Maybe."

"Let's watch the boat and see if it's him," Neal said.

"Or I could get a couple of local police, go to the boat, and take him into custody."

"We're not getting the police involved."

Piet shrugged. "I don't know if you can stop it. He stuck a fucking conch through that guy's skull."

Neal blinked. "A conch?"

"Like a big pointy seashell."

"I know what a conch is. I just—"

"You don't want to see the picture," Seo-yun interrupted.

Neal felt the blood drain from his face.

"Fuck."

"I told you I smelled something," Piet said. "Once you've smelled that . . . you don't forget it."

Seo-yun turned to the waiter and ordered the mahimahi special. Neal pushed his salad away. "Well, it doesn't help that someone was murdered, but that's not why we're here. It's not our mission." He put his napkin on the table. "I still think we just stake it out, see if it's him."

Piet folded his arms across his chest. "Is that your experience talking? You ever deal with a killer?"

Neal sighed. "I'm open to ideas."

"I can put the cops off for a day. And I doubt he'll set sail in the dark, so first thing tomorrow, we'll try it your way."

With that Piet gave Seo-yun a wink, pushed his chair back, and walked off.

Pearson had been drawing on a cocktail napkin, doodling an energized version of the bottles on the shelf, when he heard the bartender say, "You can't afford a drink here, son."

The bartender, an older Caymanian with short graying hair and a smartly trimmed mustache, reminded him of his grandfather.

"Is that so?"

"That's why I'm giving you one." The bartender placed a napkin and then a whiskey neat in front of Pearson.

"Cheers, man."

Pearson took a sip and felt the alcohol burn down his throat. It felt good. He turned and looked at the three people eating at a table nearby: the American, the Asian woman, and the midget. The bartender leaned close to Pearson.

"You want to watch out for that short fella."

"Who is he?"

"Some kind of policeman."

"The other two?"

"Work for a bank in New York."

As if on cue, the little person stood up and Pearson heard him tell his colleagues he'd see them later. Pearson watched him walk off. He had a swagger about him, that's for sure. He might be short, but like Toulouse-Lautrec, Pearson could tell he was someone you didn't wanted to fuck with.

"Why you interested?"

Pearson looked at the bartender. "Who says I am?"

The bartender shook his head. "And I gave you a free drink."

Pearson laughed. He watched the bartender polish a glass. He was surprisingly graceful for an old man, the way he moved, how he deftly worked the cloth around the shape. And he was meticulous. Probably hadn't missed a water spot or lipstick smudge in years. He was, like Pearson, an artist. Pearson realized he didn't need to confide in the bartender, didn't need to tell him anything, but there was something about this guy that inspired confidence.

"A friend of mine's gone missing. I think they have something to do with it. Or they know who did it."

"Local boy?"

Pearson nodded and knocked back the rest of the whiskey.

The bartender looked over at the table. "I do not like when people come to our island and get up to nefarious ends." He wrote down Pearson's mobile number and promised to call if he heard anything.

Piet burped. It was a spontaneous escape of gas and he tried to cover it by putting his hand over his mouth. Grover burst out laughing and pointed to his wife: "I told her, 'He's from Curaçao. Don't put too many peppers on the grouper.'"

"I like peppers."

"Your mouth might like 'em, but your belly's got other ideas."

Piet chuckled and looked at Grover's wife. She had aged well, putting on only a few pounds, but was still a lovely woman with a great laugh. "Don't listen to him. That was delicious."

Mary picked the plates off the table and looked at her husband. "Don't worry. I haven't listened to him since he got down on his knee and proposed."

"Some people only hear what they want to hear."

And then she laughed and went into the kitchen. Couples, Piet knew, often had a secret language and their own private jokes.

That kind of intimacy, a closeness that was seemingly unrelated to sex, was a mystery to him; he'd never had that experience with anyone. Who would want to marry a self-employed philanderer, a man who sometimes had anger management issues? For the first time in a long while, he felt a pang of self-pity.

"Let me fetch a couple more beers." Grover got up from the table and followed his wife into the kitchen.

Piet could hear them kissing and giggling.

Grover came back with two beers in one hand. He settled in his chair, letting gravity arrange his girth. "Now then. You want to tell me what happened in Punta Cana?"

"What do you mean?"

"A provisional warrant with your name on it came across my desk this evening."

Piet sipped his beer. "Oh, that."

"You fucked some guy up? An American? Why? You know how those people are."

Piet belched softly. "Do I need a lawyer?"

"Not yet. I'm going to do you a solid, and in return, I'm going to expect something from you."

Piet looked at the table. "I'm listening."

"Let's go back to the station. You tell me everything that's going on with this case of yours, and I'll see that the warrant finds its way to the shredder."

"And if I don't?"

Grover laughed a big, deep belly laugh. "You're funny. That's why I like you."

Bryan LeBlanc lugged the last duffel bag onto his boat. He was sweating, trying to catch his breath, but there they were: after buying the boat and putting some money in the bank, he now had ten duffel bags stacked neatly on the deck. He wiped the sweat off his face. He used to move tens of millions of dollars with just the click of a button, sending digital information flying from one server to the next in a nanosecond. This analog way of doing things was exhausting. Of course his father would've called it honest work. The irony was not lost on him.

He unlocked the hatch to the interior and walked down the companionway into the cabin. He flicked on a light and looked around. The inside was immaculate, freshly cleaned and smelling like soap. It was beautiful. Bryan smiled. He could live here. This nomadic life was going to be okay.

He noticed a bottle of wine on the table. A closer look revealed a card from Teresa thanking him for his business and wishing him bon voyage. Bryan was happy to see that she'd also written her personal number down in case he needed anything. A glass of wine sounded great, but first he had to stow the money. He'd had a locksmith put in a dead bolt for the aft cabin and he opened it. The bed had been removed, and now the cabin was simply a large storage space. A bank vault.

It didn't take long to stack the duffel bags in the room. He closed the door, locked it, and turned to the bottle of wine. He poured himself a celebratory drink. Tomorrow he would stock up on supplies, return the rental car, and, if the weather was good, set sail. He hadn't even thought about where he might go. He was just going.

Bryan had bought an iPod at the Apple store on the island and spent an afternoon loading it with music. He hooked it up to the built-in sound system and put on a genius mix of songs he'd downloaded. The playlist was called "Yacht Rock"—classic soft rock from Michael McDonald, Steely Dan, Kenny Loggins, and Seals & Crofts, plus some newer bands like Tennis, Mac DeMarco, and Toro y Moi. He figured if he was going to live like a yachtsman, he might as well go all in.

He carried his wine up the companionway onto the deck. The soft croon of Hall and Oates drifted out of the speakers. It was a pleasant tropical night. The air was warm, the sky clear and filled with stars. His boat looked beautiful, glamorous in the moonlight. He sat down at the helm seat, one hand gripping the wheel, the other holding his glass. Soft waves slopped against the hull. It would have been entirely pleasant if not for the horrible grating claxon of mating seagulls piercing the air. But Bryan didn't mind; he raised his glass and toasted the avian lovers. We should all shout like that when we're making love.

Seo-yun's phone rang again. "Always." Again. She let out a groan and sent the call to voice mail. Neal took a sip of his mojito and glanced at her. "Can I ask you a personal question?"

She looked across the patio at the swimming pool. It was quiet now; the sun had set and only a few people were in the water. She turned back to Neal. "Sure."

"Why are you getting married?"

Although she had been asking herself the same question and pondering her motives ever since that afternoon romp with the young applicant, she hadn't talked to anyone about it, had never given voice to her fears. She took a sip of her cocktail and said, "I'm just buttoning the buttons."

Neal choked on his drink. "I'm sorry?"

"It's something my parents told me. If you get the first button in the right hole, the rest will line up and the shirt will fit." She observed his reaction and continued. "Going to the right school, getting a good job—those are the first buttons. Marriage is just another one in the line."

Neal let out a sigh. "How romantic."

That made Seo-yun smile. If she were writing a summary of this trip for HR, if she wanted to be critical of her colleague, she would note that his romanticism was a flaw. He wasn't fully focused on the case, always moping around bleating about his breakup. If anyone needed to get laid—and Seo-yun couldn't remember how many times her friends had told her that, as if sex was the ultimate panacea, the all-time leading cure for whatever ails—it was Neal. Of course now that she was actually getting some, she could see what her friends were talking about; she had needed to get laid. Maybe a little sex would snap Neal out of his depression. But she didn't tell him that.

"The problem is I don't like the shirt as much as I thought I would."

"Wrong fit?"

"Wrong everything." Seo-yun's face was completely serious when she asked, "Would you care what color the tablecloths are?"

He laughed. "Yes. Very much so."

Seo-yun was pleased that she could make him laugh. It made her laugh too. She reached her cocktail out toward him and they chimed the glasses together. It was sweet, an unspoken acknowledgment of their newfound friendship.

Two patrolmen from RCIPS strolled up to them. Their white shirts with dark epaulets looked out of place in the resort, and at first Seo-yun thought they might work for one of the airlines, but the bright red stripes down the sides of their pants were the first clue that these were not commercial pilots. One of the officers said, "Neal Nathanson? Seo-yun Kim?"

Seo-yun was annoyed to hear her name mispronounced yet again. Was it really that difficult?

Neal nodded to the officers. "Yes?"

"You need to come with us."

Seo-yun looked up at the policemen. "Why? What's happened?"

"You're under arrest."

Bryan was sitting in the cockpit of his boat, pouring his second glass of wine, when he heard a voice say, "I love that song."

He stood up and saw Teresa standing on the pier. "This one?"

She nodded. "Does it get any smoother than Michael McDonald?"

"Actually, it does."

"Glad to see you're enjoying the boat, Mr. Ebanks."

"If you call me Cuffy, I'll pour you a glass of this delicious wine a really sweet person gave me."

Teresa smiled. "Glad to see you're enjoying the wine, Cuffy."

He held out a hand and she took it as she climbed into the boat. Her skin felt soft.

"Did your parents give you that name?"

Bryan ducked into the galley and grabbed another glass. He poured her some wine and winked. Bryan decided, at that moment, that Cuffy was someone who might wink at women. He was just the kind of mischievous rogue who would do that. Who knows? Some women might find it charming.

"They wanted a girl. So . . ."

She took the glass and sat on the helm seat. "So you were supposed to be Buffy?"

Bryan laughed. "I never asked." He took a sip of the wine and said, "This is delicious. Thank you."

"It's one of my favorites." Another song came on and Teresa cocked her head as she listened. "Is that the Doobie Brothers?"

"It might be Steely Dan. I'm new to the yacht-rock lifestyle."

Teresa laughed. "So this is it. You're going to spend your life riding the wind, traveling the world, living the dream."

"You make it sound like a bad thing."

She shook her head. "No way. I make my living selling the dream." She leaned back and sipped her wine. "I just think I'd get lonely."

"We can't all save the world." He said it to sound like a man resigned to his fate, as if there were something epic and worldly about his leaving the rat race, but then he realized that wasn't necessarily true. "But the truth is I've no clue what I'll do."

"It's good to keep your options open." She finished her wine and put the glass down. "When do you cast off?"

"Tomorrow morning. I still have some loose ends to tie up."

"Let me know if you need anything."

She held out her hand. Bryan shook it and then said, "I'll stop by your office to say good-bye."

She smiled. "Come by for a coffee."

Piet wasn't going to sweat it. The provisional warrant was a nuisance, but it wasn't the end of the world. The American tourist would think he'd see justice done, but Piet would trot out the entire staff of the resort to testify that the tourist was a racist blowhard who'd earned every stitch in his fucked-up face. Maybe Piet would countersue for emotional distress, add punitive damages for the ravages of colonialism to the Caribbean region. The American could be looking at a fine of a couple hundred billion dollars. Four hundred years of payback is a bitch.

The bigger problem was seeing his clients held as material witnesses in a murder investigation. It wouldn't surprise Piet if the charges suddenly escalated to potential accessories to murder, whatever the higher-ups at the RCIPS thought might give them a bigger payout. Not that they were corrupt. It was just business.

Grover entered the room and looked at him. "Oh, don't be that way."

"What way?"

"Don't pout."

Piet picked at the lip of the paper coffee cup he'd been given. The coffee was long gone. "I'm not pouting. I'm concerned about my clients."

"Don't be. They've got a lawyer coming in a few minutes."

Piet was impressed. "That was fast."

"This particular lawyer is a member of Parliament."

"Can't say I didn't warn you."

"Hey. An upstanding local turns up dead. Some Americans are poking around the dead guy's home with a private detective. I'd be derelict if I didn't look into it." Grover pulled out a chair and sat across from Piet. "I ran that name you gave me. LeBlanc."

"And?"

"Nothing. No one named LeBlanc blew in on any plane or stepped off a cruise ship. No LeBlanc staying at any hotel."

"So you drew a LeBlanc?"

Grover laughed. "How long have you been waiting to use that?"

"It just came to me."

Grover smiled. "What would make it funnier is if I shot you with a Taser right now."

Piet remembered working with Grover on an interisland case once. He recalled how the more Grover smiled, the more violent the response was about to be. Piet held up his hands. "I'm sorry, man. Sorry."

Grover's smiled faded. He relaxed back into his chair.

Piet leaned forward. "Let me talk to them, see what else I can learn. I know they went to the victim's bank. I honestly don't know why."

"Too late. The lawyer's already in there with them."

Piet crumpled the paper cup and said, "I have an idea."

The lawyer had a bow tie. Neal couldn't decide if he was impressed by the fact that the attorney got dressed in a crisply pressed suit to come see them at the police station or if he was unnerved by it. You would think someone in the tropics might play it more casual. Of course the hourly fee this guy was charging the company probably demanded formal attire. Still, he was a good-looking man in his midfifties, and Neal could tell by the way he carried himself that he was important—this was not your typical public defender. The lawyer sat at the table next to Neal and said, "I have a personal message from your boss. He says, 'Keep up the good work.'"

Neal looked at the lawyer. He wasn't sure he understood the message the CEO was trying to deliver. "I'm sorry?"

The lawyer continued. "Whatever it takes."

The lawyer flashed a thumbs-up and Neal noticed that his fingernails were professionally manicured. Neal leaned close to the attorney, close enough to catch a whiff of a dry gin martini, and said, "We didn't kill anyone."

The lawyer nodded. "Of course not."

"We didn't."

"But if you had, your boss wouldn't be upset." The lawyer held eye contact with each of them in turn. "Take that as a positive."

Neal didn't say anything. What was there to say? Seo-yun broke the silence. "Can you get my cell phone back?"

The lawyer nodded. "In due time." He then turned to Neal. "So, tell me, why are you on our beautiful island?"

Neal was unsure how much to tell him.

"Whatever you tell me is confidential. Lawyer-client privilege is extended," the lawyer reassured him.

Neal scanned the room, looking for signs of two-way mirrors or some sort of listening device. It was what he would call nondescript. Industrial beige paint seemed to cover every surface. The floor was beige linoleum, the table beige Formica. Neal wanted to laugh. This room was so nondescript it actually erased descriptors from your mind. It was anti-descript. It created a non-impression. It was tricky.

Seo-yun finally spoke up. "A broker embezzled some money. We traced it to a bank here. The guy who got murdered was the assistant manager at the bank."

The lawyer ran his fingers through his hair. "So you think the broker murdered the bank manager."

Seo-yun shook her head. "There's no way. I know him. There's just no way."

Neal turned to her. "How can you be sure?"

Seo-yun shrugged. "I'm sure."

The lawyer tapped his fingers on the table. "Who knows, right? He could be dead too. There could be a third party involved. Either way, there's no reason for you to be held. My job is to get you out of police custody."

With that the lawyer snapped his briefcase closed and left the room.

It had never occurred to Neal that he might spend the night in jail. He was a law-abiding citizen. He didn't live in a city where he might accidentally drink that one extra drink and then get behind the wheel of a car, and he didn't hang out at bars where people got into fights. It was true that he marched in political protests from time to time, but he'd never been in a riot, and if one broke out, he would get away from it as fast as he could.

Neal sat on the hard metal bench and looked around the cell. Unlike the holding room he'd been in, this room was not nondescript. Metal sink, metal toilet, metal bench, concrete walls, each bearing a grimy patina that told a story of dirt and sweat, of blood and snot and semen spattered across the surfaces and allowed to petrify. The floor was splotched and faded, some parts chemically blistered by solvents, while other areas were built up with thick rivulets of scuzzy matter. The distinct aroma of industrial cleaner mixed with an undertone of rancid feces tickled his nostrils and filled his mouth with an acrid taste. The walls revealed the artistic endeavors of previous tenants; there were layers of incomprehensible graffiti and at least a hundred crude drawings of ejaculating penises scrawled on the brick.

Neal had to admit that some of the artwork was not without charm, but there was nothing that invited erotic musings. Maybe if it was a little cleaner it could be a kind of kinky backroom fantasy, the kind of place he might've taken Bart on his birthday or something. You know, go wild. Role-play. Buy some handcuffs.

At least Seo-yun was released. The lawyer had told the police they were following up on a suspicious wire transfer and that was why they were looking for the assistant bank manager. It was just bad timing that someone murdered him. It was completely believable and yet the George Town police seemed unconvinced. So a deal was struck. He stayed in jail, Seo-yun went back to the Ritz, and the lawyer would sort it all out in the morning.

Neal put his hands behind his head and lay back on the crusty metal bench. If LeBlanc had purchased that boat he saw at the marina, well, he'd probably be sailing away soon. Not that there was much Neal could do about it from jail. He might as well try to get some sleep.

He settled in and decided that he'd throw his clothes in the trash when he got back to the hotel. He wouldn't bother sending them to the laundry. The lights in the cell went out, but it wasn't really dark; a shaft of moonlight blasted in from the window. Neal looked up at the ceiling and something caught his eye. Neal stood up on the bench for a closer look. Sure enough, it was a stalactite of dried semen dangling six or seven feet above the bench, glowing in the soft moonlight. Neal didn't think it was physically possible to launch a come load that high. Who could do that? But then there it was. It was a marvel.

"I need a drink."

Piet watched as Seo-yun headed across the Ritz-Carlton lobby. Although he felt like he'd been worked over in the police station, a drink seemed like a good idea. He followed her to the bar.

The bartender smoothed out his graying mustache with his left hand while setting two paper napkins on the bar with his right. Seo-yun looked at him and said, "Bourbon. On ice." The bartender nodded and turned to Piet. Piet smiled even though he didn't feel like smiling and scanned the bottles behind the bartender. Nothing jumped out at him, so he said, "A beer for me."

Piet sat down on the bar stool next to Seo-yun. She was trembling. "I can't believe Neal has to spend the night in jail."

Piet reached out and touched her hand. "We'll pick him up first thing in the morning."

"And then what?"

"Then we get you guys off the island."

The bartender placed their drinks in front of them and went back to tidying up the bar. It was quiet; the only other guests were a couple drinking wine. Seo-yun took a long pull of her bourbon. "What about LeBlanc?"

"I don't trust the police. They don't have any leads. I think they want to flip this whole thing around on us."

"But we didn't do it."

Piet shrugged. "Innocent people are put in jail all the time."

"But Neal just found a clue. Down at the marina."

"People buy boats here all the time."

"It's worth following up."

Piet leaned close to her. "Listen, I'm here to help with the investigation, but I need to protect you too. None of us can find LeBlanc from a jail cell." Piet watched her consider what he was saying.

"What if something happens to him in there?"

"You guys are VIPs staying at the Ritz. The concierge has probably already called the jailers and sent over some pure cotton sheets. Maybe they'll even put a chocolate on his pillow."

"We owe it to Neal to check out that boat."

Piet nodded. "We can check on the boat in the morning, on our way to the airport."

Seo-yun sipped her drink. "I'd better go work on my résumé."

"Why?"

"This is an absolute failure."

He put his hand on hers. "It's not your fault. Someone got murdered. Once that happens . . ." Piet thought about what to say. "You should go back to New York."

She sighed. "I don't want to go back. Not yet anyway."
"Come to Curaçao."
"I don't think we'll find him there."
Piet shrugged. "We can have fun while we look."
"I need more fun."

Pearson had gotten a phone tip from the bartender at the Ritz-Carlton that the American he had been watching had been arrested and was spending the night in jail. Pearson didn't really know what to do—he had no special training in abduction or murder—but he was an artist, and artists think for themselves. Seeing things differently is what creates an original work of art. Pearson would have to improvise. That's why he was waiting in his car when the American came stumbling out of the police station.

The American held his hand up to keep the morning sun out of his eyes as Pearson approached him. He seemed unsettled, as if Pearson were going to ask him for spare change or bother him somehow. "Mister? I'm here to give you a ride," Pearson said reassuringly.

"I don't know what you're talking about."

"The little man and the Asian woman sent me."

The American seemed surprised. "She's Korean American, actually."

Pearson shrugged. "You're the boss."

Saying that seemed to put the American at ease. Pearson knew it would. Pinkies always liked to be called "boss" or "chief" and hear you say, "Yes, sir, no problem, sir." One minute they feel threatened by a black man and the next they're feeling that it's all under control, the hierarchy reestablished.

The American grimaced, as if he was really torn about what to do, like he couldn't decide, but he finally made up his mind and said, "Are we going straight to the marina?"

Pearson nodded. "Straightaway."

The American relaxed. "Okay. Let's go."

Pearson opened the passenger door to his yellow Jeep and the American climbed in.

Bryan drove out to the Bay Market. He figured he'd get enough provisions for at least a week. It was exciting to be provisioning for a voyage. Even the word *provisioning* made him smile. He'd never imagined that someday he'd have a boat—his boat— that would allow him to sail away to wherever he wanted. If he wanted to go to Carnival, he could sail to Brazil. If he wanted to see some zebras, he could cross the Atlantic to Africa. He could go far and wide and never come back. It was in his best interest not to come back.

His father had talked about the need for freedom, and not that bullshit American exceptionalism that old people usually go on about. For him it was creative freedom, humanity's inalienable right to construct poems in free verse, the power to break the chains of the sestina and villanelle. He wondered if his father had felt free in his little apartment. He'd been retired, so he could have done his favorite thing: passing the time with his nose in his papers and books. But not having to work and being free seemed like two different things.

Which was why Bryan had wanted to make a statement: to declare his freedom from the tyranny of the computer monitor, his liberation from having to answer to Wall Street, a big whole-hearted fuck you to the capitalist system and all the bad karma associated with it. Call it dropping out or early retirement, but somebody had to show that those values were corrupt; exploiting people didn't lead to happiness. He could make a stand for a better world, inflict some hurt on a big bank—all that and get a tan.

His idea was to sail east along the southern coast of Cuba, past Haiti, the Dominican Republic, and Puerto Rico, heading for the Lesser Antilles. Get as far away from the Caymans as possible. Who knows, if the weather held he might try to cross the Atlantic and get to the Mediterranean.

He parked on Market Street and went inside.

Bay Market was fancy, with lots of imported goods displayed under spotlights as if they were diamonds. It made sense; it wasn't easy to import gourmet food from Europe to a small island, so you'd want to showcase it, but it created a somber shopping experience. Not that he was complaining—the air-conditioning was rocking.

As he perused the gourmet cheese selection he began to relax. There was something reassuring about the Manchego and Camembert and chèvre, like being back in his old life in New York City, standing in Dean & DeLuca, looking at fancy foods flown halfway around the world for his pleasure. He grabbed several different kinds of cheese. Everything was going to be fine. He felt optimistic for the first time in months. He was setting sail. It was all working out. He'd be off the coast of Cuba by the end of the day. Maybe he'd pull into port and buy a cigar.

Seo-yun sat in the car while Piet went into the police station to get Neal. She watched him walk into the station. He had a strut. She liked that. And even if he wasn't as tall as most people, he was sexy. There was just something about him. He knew exactly what she wanted before she knew it. He understood her desires. Maybe that's because he was an experienced lover.

It's not that she was so experienced; she'd had only a handful of boyfriends and, until recently, hadn't really slept around. Maybe she hadn't taken a big enough sample to make a valid finding, but from her limited exposure to the sexual skills of men, Piet was in a league of his own. Or maybe they clicked. She'd heard that sometimes people clicked, but the whole thing seemed like a myth, something people said to justify marriage and children. It suddenly occurred to her that her fiancé might want to procreate with her. She tried to imagine little emo-haired toddlers running amok in her apartment, demanding juice boxes, shitting in their pants, and scattering Cheerios everywhere. The babies would want to feed on her. They would squall and holler until she let them suck milk out of her breasts like little vampires. She shuddered. The whole thing made her skin crawl.

Piet wasn't gone long. She watched him come out of the police station and get into the driver's seat.

"Where's Neal?"

"They released him an hour ago."

Piet seemed concerned, so she tried to reassure him. "I'm sure he's fine." Seo-yun reached for her phone. "I'll call him."

"I'm getting away from here."

Piet put the car in gear and drove slowly away from the station. Seo-yun looked at her phone. "Voice mail."

"This doesn't feel right."

"He could've taken a cab."

Piet shook his head. "I really hope they didn't decide to take some initiative."

"What does that mean?"

"It means that if the police figure out he's after someone with a bunch of money, then they might do whatever they need to do to find the guy with the money."

"You think they'd hurt him?"

"I'm just saying that we should get the hell out of here."

The drove in silence for a moment as Seo-yun thought about what Piet was saying. Were they in danger? Would the police torture Neal and steal the money? Or was Piet trying to get them off the island because he wanted the money for himself? And how could anyone do anything until LeBlanc was found? What if LeBlanc was dead?

"Why would they do that?"

Piet glanced at her. "For the same reason your guy stole the money in the first place."

Seo-yun didn't know why LeBlanc stole the money. She thought she knew him, thought they were colleagues, but then this happened and now she wondered if she ever really knew him. She realized she could say the same thing about herself. She thought she knew who she was and what she wanted, she thought she had her life all figured out, and then she surprised herself. How did that happen? Were people inherently insane?

Piet touched her arm. "You okay?"

She wasn't okay. She didn't know how to feel, exactly. It was all confusing, and confusion was something she usually cut through with logic. She muttered, "Money doesn't buy happiness."

Piet patted her hand. "People without money don't know that."

His trunk full of groceries—bags of gourmet cheeses, instant ramen, cans of tuna, tomato sauce, pasta, garbanzo beans, and six bottles of pinot grigio—Bryan LeBlanc drove into the marina parking lot and pulled to a stop. He was still feeling good, buoyant even. The ship was ready; the cash was stowed and secure. He'd swung by the bank this morning and deposited another half million dollars in Cuffy's bank account just in case anything went haywire. All he needed to do was stock the galley with provisions—the extra-virgin olive oil and balsamic vinegar, the sea salt and pepper jelly—and then he could cast off and begin his new life as a wandering person of leisure or whatever it was he was about to become.

What was he going to do? Float around the world eating cheese and reading books? Not that it was such a bad thing to do. Maybe he could do some charity work. Invest in some local schemes. Help a fisherman buy a new net or pay for a young woman to go to college in the US. That could be worthwhile. Make him feel less like a parasite without totally depleting his cash. He'd have to figure out how to disburse the funds, but Cuffy Ebanks's floating microloan savings and trust sounded like a cool idea. Or maybe he'd write an anonymous memoir: a how-to for ripping off Wall Street.

A marina workman came out with a cart to help haul the supplies to his boat. As they were unloading the trunk, Teresa walked out of the office.

"Got time for a coffee?"

Bryan smiled. "The weather looks good for sailing. I think I should take advantage."

Teresa ran her fingers through her hair and said, "I was hoping I could lure you to my house for dinner before you left."

Their eyes locked, and for a brief moment, Bryan was tempted to say yes, but then the feeling of being so close to accomplishing everything made him look away.

"I know, it's a bit sudden." A wry smile played on her lips.

Bryan shook his head. "It's not that. It's just . . ."

"The FBI are closing in."

He laughed and then immediately regretted it, because it sounded like a fake laugh, a nervous laugh. "Can I take a rain check?"

"Only if you'll use it."

Bryan smiled. "It is with the best intentions that I take your rain check."

Teresa smiled back. "I'm kind of surprised our paths haven't crossed before. We're about the same age. It's a small island."

She was right, of course she was. Fortunately, he'd already given this line of questioning some thought. "I grew up in the States."

"And you never came for a visit? You must have some relatives here."

Bryan nodded. "My parents had some falling-out with their families. I think they didn't approve of their marriage. They never talked about it."

"Perhaps an unexpected pregnancy was the cause."

Bryan laughed. "Yep. It's all my fault." He looked around. "Although I do wish I had grown up here."

"Well, you're here now."

In that moment he calculated the risks versus the rewards of staying, even if only for dinner, and quickly realized that it would be impossible for him to be with her. He had murdered someone on this island; he couldn't be coming back for visits, hanging around, or getting involved in a romance. Sooner or later someone—the police or Leighton's angry friend—was going to figure it out, and then he'd be fucked.

"It was really great to meet you."

Teresa nodded. "Pleasure doing business, Mr. Ebanks."

Neal was impressed. Sure, there were some cheesy-looking paintings of sea turtles, done in the kind of fluorescent pastels you'd find in a Fort Lauderdale hotel room, but there were other works that wouldn't look out of place at a gallery in Chelsea. They were in some kind of ramshackle boat barn turned into a studio: tubes of paint lined up on a rough wood table, brushes resting in a rusted yellow Café Bustelo can, and a few blank canvases leaning against the walls. Paintings were everywhere, in stacks on a table, propped on chairs, hanging from nails on the wall; a half-finished painting of a pod of dolphins breaching waves at sunset stood on an easel in the center of the room.

"These are really good." Neal smiled. "But shouldn't we get going? Aren't we meeting the others at the marina?"

"I just need to pick something up."

Pearson shot him a look. There was some tough-guy posturing behind it. Neal felt his face flush. The artist was lean and strong and mysterious. There was something dangerous about him: the way he carried himself, the muscular curve of his ass as he bent over a table. Neal could imagine what happened next: a hot and heavy session in the studio of a handsome artist on a tropical island. That sounded like one of Joe Gage's films; instead of *L.A. Tool & Die* it could be *Cayman Cock & Canvas*.

Neal felt his penis begin to stir. He adjusted his posture—he'd been standing in what he thought might be a provocative pose, leaning against a wall, hips jutting forward, but now he felt slightly embarrassed.

"Time is of the essence." Neal couldn't believe he'd just coughed up such a cliché, but it seemed to work. Pearson nodded and picked up an object from underneath a table. Neal saw that he was holding a wooden-handled thing with a sharp, barbed point on the end. "What's that?"

"A gun for spearfishing."

"Are we going fishing?"

"In a manner."

The sudden appearance of a weapon made Neal feel uncomfortable. "I'm not sure that's necessary."

Pearson shrugged. "Depends on what happens when we find the money."

The two men looked at each other for a long beat. Pearson held the speargun at an angle, not really pointing it at Neal but not really not pointing it at him either.

Neal cleared his throat. "Sure. That's probably right."

"Do you know where the money is?"

Neal shook his head. It was dawning on him that perhaps the artist was not working for Piet. "I don't."

The artist's expression changed. He looked disappointed. For some reason Neal felt the need to elaborate.

"I'm trying to find it. But to be clear, the money belongs to the bank I work for."

Pearson shrugged. "Maybe Mr. Spear will say different."

Seo-yun pointed to a sign on a big white building. "There it is."

Piet pulled the car into the marina parking lot just as Seo-yun saw her former colleague, Bryan LeBlanc, talking to a woman in front of the marina office. She let out a little yelp and ducked her head into Piet's lap.

Piet put his hand on her head and gently pressed her face into his crotch. "I like driving with you, baby."

Seo-yun lifted her head. "Cut it out. That's him."

Piet scanned the lot as he nonchalantly parked the car. He saw a man who looked like LeBlanc hugging a woman in white jeans.

"You sure?"

Seo-yun popped up and then ducked back down. "Positive."

"Stay down."

Seo-yun felt Piet's penis begin to swell in his pants. She looked up at him. "Really?"

He shrugged. "I like you." He turned the engine off and watched as LeBlanc walked down the pier. "The coast is clear."

She sat up. "That was close."

They opened their doors and got out of the car, trying to act natural, as if they weren't following anyone, although Seo-yun did notice the bulge in Piet's trousers and it made her smile. As they started walking toward the pier, Atlantic Starr began playing in her purse. "Shit."

"He can recognize you. Stay in the car and lie low."

She watched as he trotted off in LeBlanc's direction and then she answered her phone. "What?" She listened for a moment and then said, "Please don't call me bae. It means 'shit' in Danish. Did you know that? Who wants to be called shit?" She held the phone away from her ear, letting her fiancé's nasal voice blare into the humid tropical air. Finally she said, "I'm sure grilled salmon will be fine."

She hung up. He'd said, "I love you" about nineteen times before signing off. She knew he'd needed her to say it back to him, to let him hear a reassuring echo, but she didn't want to say it.

She did love him in a way. He wasn't a bad person, he meant well, and he adored her, but he was so annoying. Seo-yun didn't know why, but denying him the "I love you"—knowing that it drove him crazy, turned him into a puddle of neurotic need and desperate clinginess—turned her on. She liked having the power.

She saw Piet round the corner and jog toward her as fast as he could while still appearing nonchalant.

Piet hated running. It was one thing that he just couldn't do. He was an excellent swimmer and an avid cyclist, but running hurt his legs and had the added humiliation of looking comical. Being laughed at could really set him off. *You think it's funny being born with achondroplasia? Really?*

Fuuuuuuck you.

Piet hated running and Christmas. He hated Santa Claus or Saint Nicholas or whatever you wanted to call the bearded guy in the red suit. In the Dutch tradition Saint Nicholas had an assistant named Zwarte Piet, a black elf who was either Santa's little helper or his little enslaved person, depending on your point of view. Piet was black and short and named Piet, so Christmas was the time of year when he was subjected to a steady stream of racist and heightist insults and slurs that he was supposed to endure with a smile on his face. No one meant any harm. People were just joking. Just being jolly.

He didn't celebrate Christmas. And he tried not to run unless it was absolutely necessary.

Which was why he and Seo-yun walked down the pier in the direction of LeBlanc's boat.

"It's the boat on the end. Down there."

Seo-yun shielded her eyes. "Nice boat."

"I think you should wait here. I'll go subdue him."

"Subdue him?"

Piet was annoyed that she wasn't following his orders. After all, he had experience in these kinds of things. "Yeah. He's dangerous."

Seo-yun laughed. "Bryan?"

"Somebody put a conch through that guy's head."

"No way am I waiting here. This is the exciting part."

Piet gritted his teeth. People didn't like to get caught, they put up a fight, and he figured he'd probably have to fuck this guy up, but he didn't tell her about that. "This bit is never as exciting as you think."

They were only about halfway down the pier when Piet saw LeBlanc cast off and putter out of the marina toward the open ocean. Piet pointed. Seo-yun squinted at the boat as it turned down the channel. She raised her hand like a schoolgirl who knew the answer and waved at the boat. For some reason LeBlanc turned and gave her a wave in return.

"What's that about?"

Seo-yun shrugged. "I'm not sure."

She watched the sleek sailboat make another turn and head for open water. Piet grabbed her arm and said, "This isn't over."

He walked off toward a kiosk that was offering parasailing lessons.

When Bryan saw Seo-yun standing on the pier with what looked like a dwarf, he nearly shit himself. They had come so close to catching him. If he'd gone to dinner at Teresa's—hell, if he'd bothered to shave this morning—he'd now be sitting in some office trying to explain himself while they carted all the money back to the bank. He'd barely had a chance to stow his gourmet cheeses.

He steered through the marina, past fishing boats, the occasional catamaran, a few speedboats tied to the dock, a Jet Ski rental place. He was annoyed with himself. He'd meticulously left false trails and fake clues, and still they'd almost caught him. He must have made a mistake somewhere along the line, underestimated Seo-yun, or gotten careless. Maybe he left a clue on his computer. He felt a cold chill race up his spine. If he'd been sloppy enough for them to find him, then maybe they'd figured out he murdered Leighton. Maybe they'd already told the Cayman police.

The boat motored out of the marina and Bryan was able to crank the throttle and pick up speed as he headed out to sea. He saw the wind vane on top of the mast catch the breeze. There was a strong gust coming from the south.

He fumbled a bit undoing the strap, then checked that the halyard was attached to the sail and began winching the rope, raising the sail. It caught the wind immediately and blew the boat sideways until he could reach the rudder and get it going in the right direction. From there he trimmed the sails and the boat began to pick up speed. He considered trying to pull out the asymmetrical spinnaker, but that might be too much; he hadn't practiced hoisting the sails on this boat and was unsure of all the connections. He'd raise the jib as soon as he got a bit farther offshore. Right now he needed to get out into international waters.

He wondered if InterFund would press charges. He'd always assumed they wouldn't; they'd have to extradite him and he'd make sure it got into the news cycle. It would have been terrible for client confidence, but who knows, nowadays corporations hired PR firms to spin the most lurid shit into gossamer. Maybe they would try to put him in jail for a million years.

But they hadn't caught him yet. With a strong breeze and a head start, he could get out on the open ocean and be hard to find. By night he could get to Cuba, where there were lots of little coves and harbors to hide in. He still had a chance.

Seo-yun had called Neal and told him they'd seen Bryan sailing away. When Neal relayed this to Pearson, he drove his yellow Jeep to the marina, taking corners like a maniac.

When they got there, Piet was waiting in a speedboat with the engine idling. Neal saw Seo-yun waving frantically. He started to jog toward her but heard Pearson say, "Take it easy." Neal felt the tip of the speargun prod his lower back and so he slowed down, letting the painter set the pace.

Seo-yun was standing by the boat, talking into her phone. She shouted, "He's getting away. Come on." She didn't seem to notice the guy walking with him. The guy with the speargun in his hands.

He turned toward Pearson. "Stop poking me with that thing."

Pearson didn't say anything; he just poked Neal again and this time drew blood. Neal could feel a drop or two forming on his skin and slowly rolling down his back toward his buttocks. Unless that was sweat. It was crushingly hot out. But then sweating doesn't begin with a sharp pain, so he probably was bleeding, not profusely or anything, just enough to require a tetanus booster.

Seo-yun started shouting at her cell phone. Neal heard her say something about tablecloths and not giving a fuck what color they were.

"Stop fucking around." The sound of Pearson's voice and a firm jab with the speargun snapped Neal to attention.

Piet revved the engine of the speedboat, causing it to buck and strain against the ropes, and shouted at Neal. "Come on!"

Seo-yun hung up her phone and climbed into the speedboat.

When Piet saw Pearson coming up behind Neal, he said, "Who's that?"

"He's an artist."

"We don't need an artist."

Pearson shoved Neal into the speedboat, a move that revealed the speargun, and hopped in next to him. Neal saw a flash of concern on Piet's face. "Oh. That kind of artist."

Pearson turned to Piet. "Where are we going?"

Piet glared at him. "What's it to you?"

Pearson pointed the speargun at Piet's crotch. "If I were you I'd stop asking questions and drive the boat."

Piet looked at Neal and said, "Unhook the fucking rope."

Marinas have speed limits, but Piet didn't care; he opened up the throttle and the twin Mercury motors began viciously churning the water. The acceleration threw Neal back against the side of the hull, slamming the spot where he'd already been poked by the speargun. He watched the speedboat's wake hit the boats that were docked and set them rocking side to side as if they were on a gimbal. He heard a few angry shouts over the roar of the motors as the front of the boat lifted and they shot out toward the open ocean, hitting the waves with jolting thuds. He glanced at Seo-yun and saw she had a smile on her face, as if this was fun.

Farther out, past the break, the boat settled into a steady thrum. Neal tapped Pearson on the shoulder. "I'm prepared to offer you a substantial reward for your help today."

Pearson laughed. "That's very nice of you. Thank you." He turned to Piet. "Where would we be without the kindness of pinkies?"

Neal looked at both men and, for the first time, wondered if they were in some kind of alliance.

Piet handed Neal a pair of binoculars. "Keep an eye on the sailboat."

Seo-yun wished she'd listened to her dad and kept taking Tae Kwon Do classes. Then maybe she could let out a ferocious *kihap* and leap into a spinning, flying kick to the head of the guy with the speargun. Snap his neck and send him flying overboard. But she couldn't do any of that; she'd stopped taking lessons when she was eight, preferring math and computer games to anything requiring human contact. She hardly remembered how to throw a punch. She decided that when she got back to the city, she'd enroll in self-defense classes. It would be good to learn some technique and get a little exercise, get out of the house more.

Seo-yun liked being outside. She liked being out on the water. The air was fresh and clean, and the sun warmed her skin. Her body felt good. Her mind was alert. She felt alive. Best of all, her cell phone didn't get any reception. Her hair whipped across her face and spray from a wave blew over her. Why did she work so hard to create a life spent entirely indoors? What had she been thinking?

She looked off at the sailboat. It appeared to be getting closer. It wasn't much of a chase, really. Bryan had nowhere to hide and they had the advantage of engine power. Still, sometimes his boat looked farther away than it was. It was hard to tell.

What would she say when they caught him? Was she going to scold him? *How could you betray your fiduciary duty?* Tell him she had no choice but to write up a negative performance review in his personnel file? Or would she take him aside and tell him that she admired what he'd done: he'd taken a chance, he'd broken free. She kind of felt like giving him a high five.

The idea of going back to New York—days spent in the office breathing filtered air and the toxic off-gassing of thousands of computer servers churning data, and nights in her austere apartment eating takeout with her fiancé—was too much. Returning to Wall Street and the life she had, just thinking about it, caused her throat to clench. And that's when it occurred to her that she didn't have to go back.

Piet squinted off at the horizon.

Neal pointed toward a sailboat out ahead of them. "I think that's him."

It was hard to say; they weren't close enough to make a positive ID. Piet tapped Neal's arm. "Give me those for a second." Neal handed him the binoculars. Piet tried to get a visual, but the powerboat was bouncing too much. Even looking for a few seconds caused his stomach to lurch.

While they stood at the wheel, Neal leaned in and tried to whisper above the whine of the engines and the hiss of the hull cutting through the ocean. "What do you think? Can we take him?"

Piet didn't respond.

"He's got to reload it, right? He can only shoot one of us at a time."

Piet turned to Neal. "After he shoots you, I'll jump him while he's trying to reload. Is that your plan?"

"That's not what I had in mind."

Neal moved off to the side. Piet turned the powerboat a few degrees, trying to find an angle to intercept the sailboat. This kind of thing—the heroic gesture, the "Let's kick their ass while they're reloading"—this was what amateurs did. They watched a bunch of movies, thought they had the reflexes of a ninja and just needed the right moment to make their move. Of course when they did, the next thing they knew there's a spear sticking out of their forehead. Cause of death: stupid Hollywood movies. Piet wished he could give Neal some advice: stay out of the way and let a professional deal with this. Not that Piet had any great ideas about how to disarm the guy. Sometimes the smartest thing to do was play it out. See where things went. It wasn't heroic, but it was better than pulling a harpoon out of your neck. Nobody was going to get hurt until they found LeBlanc and the money. Then things would get interesting. Heroic action might need to be taken. Right now the best plan Piet could think of was to let Neal antagonize the guy until he fired his spear, and then that would be the right moment to do something. It would be even better if LeBlanc got skewered. Best would be if they all killed each other and he and Seo-yun could take the money and go away together.

Piet sighed. He really was a romantic at heart.

Pearson thought about Winslow Homer, J. M. W. Turner, and Hokusai. They were great painters of water. But so were Claude Monet and Emil Nolde. Their work was different in style and tone, but each of them understood something about how to see. They got it. Among contemporary painters, David Hockney was the master of the splash and ripple, no contest, and Pearson was a big fan of his work. But Hockney mostly painted swimming pools. The ocean was a whole different beast. It was a shame that so many paintings of seascapes were lame. It was always a glint of sunset and a touch of white on the cresting waves; there was never any depth, no appreciation for the power of the ocean. Pearson had a lot of practice painting seascapes, although most of them were cheesy sunsets with happy dolphins and splashing whale flukes. But he loved painting the ocean, it was a beautiful thing to do—technically challenging too, the way the sun refracted off the waves, the surface shifting and changing; that kind of light and movement was extremely hard to evoke in a two-dimensional oil painting.

A painting by Gustave Caillebotte came to his mind. It wasn't a seascape. It was called *Les raboteurs de parquet* and it was probably his favorite. It was perfect. He aspired to paint like that. Every detail was sublime: the light streaming through the window, the stripes of the wood, the way the muscles of the men scraping the floor revealed motion and energy, the bottle of wine by the fireplace, the way Caillebotte balanced the figures in the frame, the palette—it was a painting that fired on all cylinders. It was hanging in the Musée d'Orsay in Paris. He could go see it. He could go see all the art.

Pearson watched the American lean close to the little person and whisper. He tightened his grip on the speargun. They were probably planning something, some attempt to overpower him. He expected it. He was ready. The job wasn't done. He didn't have the money yet. As Pablo Picasso famously said, "Art washes away from the soul the dust of everyday life." That was a good thing. He would need a lot of art, because it was about to get real dusty in his soul.

Bryan watched the powerboat slowly closing the space between them. It was almost imperceptible yet relentless, like watching a swimming pool fill one drop at a time. Unless they ran out of fuel or their engines broke down, or some magic wind picked him up and carried him away, they were eventually going to catch him.

And then what? Would they try to arrest him? He was in international waters now, and even if they had policemen with them, they had no jurisdiction. They would want to recover the money, but again, they had no legal recourse. There was always the very real possibility they would resort to piracy—keelhaul him, make him walk the plank, or just drag him back to George Town in handcuffs.

Maybe he could cut a deal. Bryan started to think about his negotiating positions. He could give them all the cash and keep the boat. He still had over a million dollars in Cuffy's bank account. It wouldn't keep him financially secure forever, but it was more than most people in the world had and, with compound interest and a low-key lifestyle, he might be able to get by just fine. He'd start by demanding to keep the boat and $5 million and let them haggle him down. Then they could go home victorious. It was a win-win.

Bryan was surprised that he didn't feel panicked or scared or angry. What a strange sensation. The embezzlement had been a big idea, a bold plan that he'd managed to, until this new wrinkle, pull off. Knowing he'd done that gave him a sense of satisfaction that was hard to define. But then killing Leighton had ruined everything. It really had.

Neal didn't know if they would ever close the gap between their powerboat and the white dot on the horizon, but eventually the sleek sailboat came into full view. Neal could see that LeBlanc had the wind at his back, attempting to outrun them. He checked the gas gauge on the powerboat and looked at Piet.

"A quarter of a tank?"

Piet shot him an irritated look. "I didn't have time to fill up the tank."

"Do we have enough?"

Piet shrugged. "If the wind picks up, we'll run out of gas before we catch him."

The idea that they might be stuck in the ocean, out of gas and out of luck, and with LeBlanc so close, sent a surge of panic through Neal. "But then what? We're just going to float around the ocean?"

"Then we call the Joint Marine Unit to come rescue us."

Pearson seemed to have overheard them and moved toward Seo-yun. He stuck the speargun under her chin and looked at Piet. "We are not calling the police."

Neal scowled at Pearson. "Leave her alone."

Pearson smiled. Neal wanted to say something more, to make sure Pearson understood that he wouldn't allow him to spear Seo-yun. He didn't know why, but he felt like saying she was innocent or not a part of this, but that wasn't true. She was a part of it. Still, he wanted to protect her somehow, even though he didn't have to. Piet cut the motors and let the powerboat slosh in its wake. Pearson turned and glared at Piet. "What are you doing?"

Piet stepped away from the wheel. "Not her."

"Or what? What're you gonna do?"

Piet and Pearson eyed each other, and Neal could tell that Piet was really trying to control his temper. The boat drifted, the engines idling. Neal heard waves smacking into the hull, violently rocking the boat from side to side. Behind Pearson, in the distance, he saw clouds moving overhead as the wind seemed to pick up. Neal wanted to say something, to intervene in some way. He locked eyes with Seo-yun, but it seemed that she was having an out-of-body experience.

Piet repeated himself. "Not her."

Neal tried to back Piet up. "Be reasonable."

Pearson stared at Neal and then Piet. He seemed to be trying to make a decision. Finally he lowered the speargun and said, "Let's go then."

Piet turned back to the wheel and opened up the throttle.

Neal was impressed. It turned out that Piet was something of an expert powerboat pilot. The wind seemed to have died down, or perhaps LeBlanc didn't know how to take full advantage of what wind there was. They slowly gained on him and then, almost shockingly, they pulled up alongside LeBlanc's boat without the hulls even touching. Pearson was the first to make the jump into the sailboat, followed by Seo-yun, Piet, and then Neal. LeBlanc sat with his hand on the wheel and the wind blowing through his hair, seemingly enjoying the beautiful day at sea, amused at the arrival of what Neal decided might be the strangest posse in history. For some reason the Hall and Oates song "Sara Smile" was playing on the boat's sound system. It surprised Neal, temporarily threw him off balance. Bart had been a huge Hall and Oates fan. There was no way LeBlanc could've known that. It was just serendipity.

Neal looked at Seo-yun and said, "Bart loves this song." But if she heard him, she didn't respond. She was looking at LeBlanc.

Piet turned to Neal and said, "Tie her off."

"What?"

"Tie the fucking . . ." Piet pointed at the speedboat, but it had drifted about twenty feet from the sailboat, which was continuing along as if nothing had changed. He threw his hands up in exasperation. "Oh, for fuck's sake . . ."

Neal felt a flash of anger. "Why is that my job? I'm not a nautical person."

Piet glared at Neal and said something that sounded like *"Bai chupa patin."*

Neal didn't know what that meant, but it didn't sound good and it felt like the final straw. He was about to lose his shit, about to throw a tantrum. He'd reached his limit—the stress of the chase, the night in jail, the weird sexual energy between Piet and Seo-yun, the artist with the speargun—it was all too much. Had Piet forgotten who was working for whom? He reminded himself to take a breath. Anger never helped and it wasn't going to be helpful now. He needed to keep cool. Neal tried to reassure Piet. "I'll expense the boat. Don't worry."

Piet was about to respond when Pearson reminded them he was there by pointing the speargun at LeBlanc and saying, "Where's the money?"

LeBlanc smiled. "In the aft cabin." He reached into his pocket and handed a key to Pearson. "There's also some chilled Petit Chablis and a selection of gourmet cheeses in the fridge if you're feeling hungry." LeBlanc turned to Seo-yun and smiled. "Soy? Would you mind opening the wine?"

Seo-yun nodded. "I could use a drink."

Neal sat down across from LeBlanc. Normally when he finally caught up to a scofflaw he'd feel a sense of satisfaction, of justice being served, karma ripening, scores settled, scales balanced, but looking at LeBlanc, he didn't feel any of that. He just felt numb.

LeBlanc smiled at Neal. "I had heard you were good at your job. Sorry we never met at the office."

Neal didn't know what to say, so he didn't say anything.

"Where did I mess up?"

"A deleted text message."

LeBlanc grimaced, then laughed and shook his head. "Damn."

"And give her credit, she unraveled a couple of your trades."

LeBlanc sighed. "She's good."

Neal couldn't help himself; he said, "Looks like it's game over."

LeBlanc looked at him. "I doubt the game is even in the second half."

Neal didn't know what he was talking about. How could this guy sit there and act as though nothing was happening? Maybe he wouldn't go to jail, but Neal was taking the money back. Although now that he thought about it, the guy with the speargun needed to be dealt with. That might prove to be a tricky negotiation. But then everyone has his price. He was confident that the artist wouldn't want to be responsible for a massacre. If it cost the firm a million dollars, at least he would have recovered most of it. He might not be able to bring LeBlanc to justice, but the CEO would be happy enough that he didn't get away with it.

Seo-yun came back with the bottle and some glasses. She poured the wine. "Nice boat."

LeBlanc took a glass. "Not as fast as I'd hoped."

Piet stood there, staring at them. LeBlanc turned to Piet. "And who are you?"

Piet didn't respond, so Seo-yun said, "His name is Piet. He's a private dick."

LeBlanc said, "Of course he is." Then he raised his glass. "To Wall Street."

Neal tasted the wine. It was cool and refreshing with a hint of melon and citrus. He gave LeBlanc a knowing smile. "Nice minerality." Seo-yun and LeBlanc exchanged a glance. Neal shrugged. "I learned that in a class."

Seo-yun tasted her wine and looked around. "I could get used to this."

They sat there for a moment, enjoying the wind and the sun, the fresh air, the sound of the boat cutting through the water. It was nice, like being on vacation. Neal realized that he needed some time off. He was going to put in for some vacation as soon as he got back to the office.

"Where's the guy with the speargun?" Seo-yun asked Piet.

"He's counting the money."

LeBlanc drained his glass and said, "And trying to decide how many of us he has to kill to keep it."

Neal stood. "I'm going to see what he's up to."

Neal found Pearson in the aft cabin, lying on the floor in a pile of money, muttering names of famous painters. Neal recognized a few of the artists Pearson invoked—Monet and Manet, obviously, but also Bonnard, Morisot, and Biva—then came the names he didn't recognize.

"Are you going to start collecting art?"

Pearson laughed. "This time next year I'll be in a *bistrot* on Saint-Germain drinking wine with my French girlfriend."

"You have a French girlfriend?"

"I will. A beautiful woman with a nice handbag and clean hair. One who wears stripes all the time."

Neal didn't know what that meant. "Stripes?"

"Horizontal stripes are very French."

"I've been to Paris and I don't remember seeing people wearing a lot of stripes."

Pearson's smile faded. "Their flag has stripes."

Neal realized that he was annoying the artist, that this was not going to push the conversation where it needed to be pushed. "You're right. That's absolutely true."

Pearson picked up a handful of cash and tossed it in the air.

Neal smiled. "Okay. Well, tell you what. Let's turn this boat around, go back to George Town, and I'll let you walk with two of these bags, no questions asked."

"I count ten bags."

"Right. But that money belongs to the bank. If you take it all, you're stealing. If I give you some, you earned it."

"That's not your bank's money anymore. If I'm stealing, I'm stealing from a stealer."

Neal held up his hands. "Three bags. You can live for years in Paris on that. But that's the best I can do."

Pearson let loose a full-throated guffaw and then punched Neal in the stomach with so much force that Neal just folded in on himself, crumpling to the floor as if his bones had been knocked out of his body. Pearson stood over Neal and shook his head. "Three bags."

Seo-yun didn't think it was such a good idea when Neal decided to walk into the cabin to check on the guy with the speargun. What was he going to do? Reason with him? Offer some kind of deal? That was the Wall Street way: the art of the deal or whatever. But then it's not often you go into a negotiation with a guy holding a speargun. Usually it's just lawyers in power suits sitting around a conference table, letting the billable hours pile up until someone blinks.

Piet was sitting on the other side of the cockpit from her, next to LeBlanc, who was still at the wheel, guiding the boat away from the Caymans. She jerked her head at Piet. "Shouldn't you check on Neal?"

Piet shrugged. "He's a big boy. He can handle himself."

LeBlanc laughed. "You'd be surprised. Money does funny things to people." The laugh surprised Seo-yun. Usually LeBlanc was low-key, but the sound of his laugh had an edge.

"What do you mean?" Seo-yun asked.

"Worse than anything they do on Wall Street."

Seo-yun looked at Piet, trying to convey a sense of urgency with her expression, but Piet seemed pensive, as if he was trying to figure out the next move. Another song played on the sound system. Seo-yun recognized it. "Is this Steely Dan?"

LeBlanc raised an eyebrow. "Kenny Loggins maybe?"

Seo-yun got up and sat next to him. "Can I ask you something?"

LeBlanc sipped his wine. "Of course."

"Why'd you do it? You had everything."

"The mistake is thinking that money is everything."

"So now what?"

LeBlanc checked the sail and made an adjustment, then looked at Seo-yun. "Wait and see how the story ends."

He sat back down and corrected the course—adjusting a few degrees to maximize the wind—and then cranked the sail to tighten it up.

Seo-yun wondered if that's why she was, as her fiancé said, acting out. But she just wanted to live on her own terms. There were probably people who would say that promiscuity in the face of her impending nuptials was wrong. And she recognized that it was a betrayal, that there were rules in organized relationships and society. She had never broken the rules before—she'd always been a dutiful daughter, a model employee, an ideal girlfriend—but now that she had stepped outside the lines, it felt good to be herself, to do what she wanted when she wanted. The rules seemed to be made to keep her from following her desires, from living the life that felt right. So she broke some rules. *Is that so wrong?* Was LeBlanc so wrong?

"Do you regret it?"

"If you fill up my wineglass I'll give you a critique of advanced capitalism."

That made Seo-yun laugh. "Marcuse and the Frankfurt school? No thanks. But I'll top you up."

She reached for the bottle and emptied what was left into his glass.

"Cheers."

Seo-yun was about to clink her glass against his when she heard a loud noise from the cabin. She turned to see the guy with the speargun emerge. Piet gave her a discreet shake of the head, as if he was trying to say, Don't do anything.

Bryan looked up at the wind vane. "Ah, the wind keeps shifting." He turned the crank and trimmed the sail.

The man with the speargun walked toward Bryan and said, "Turn the boat around. We're going back to George Town."

Bryan sipped his wine. He didn't move.

"Turn it around."

"We're close to Cuba. And I've always wanted to have a medianoche at midnight in Havana."

"We're going back." The man gripped the speargun and stepped closer.

Bryan shook his head and said, "If only it were that easy."

Seo-yun was surprised that Bryan was being defiant and even more surprised when the guy pulled the trigger. The spear flew across the deck and hit Bryan in the chest. Seo-yun heard a scream jump out of her mouth. The spear knocked Bryan off balance and he tumbled backward, falling into the water.

Seo-yun stood, unsure what to do next.

Piet used the distraction to bum-rush the guy with the spear-gun and slam into him. The guy stumbled, took a couple of steps, tripped over the railing, and fell into the water with a splash.

Piet grabbed the wheel and kept the sailboat moving quickly away.

"Bryan!" Seo-yun looked out over the water but didn't see anyone. No one was trying to swim or waving in distress. There were no signs of life at all. The ocean was quiet—just the sound of the wind ruffling the sails and the soft churn of the water under the hull.

She turned and could see the dim outline of an island on the horizon. That must be Cuba. That's where Bryan wanted to get a sandwich. It was a kooky idea: steal millions of dollars, buy a boat, get a sandwich. But she knew that the sandwich was more than a sandwich; it was the freedom to express your desire to get a sandwich and then fulfill it, even if it seemed silly. That's what LeBlanc had been after. That's what would make a Cuban sandwich in Cuba taste so delicious.

Seo-yun realized she was still holding her glass and reflexively sipped her wine. What else could she do?

Piet wondered if Seo-yun was in shock. Sometimes when people witnessed violence or trauma they became numb, unable to feel anything, unable to think clearly. He couldn't tell what she was thinking or what she was feeling. She stood on the deck sipping her wine, the wind whipping her hair.

Finally she said, "Shouldn't we go back and get Bryan?"

Piet shook his head. "He's dead."

"What about the other guy?"

"Fuck him."

Seo-yun said, "I'm going to go check on Neal."

"Better let me. I'm pretty sure that guy murdered him. He was going to kill us all."

She didn't say anything. She looked stunned.

Piet touched her hand. "You okay?"

"I don't know. I don't think I should be okay, should I?"

"You're alive." Seo-yun didn't respond. Piet gave her a kiss on the cheek. "That's something." He stood up. "Take the wheel. I'll go check on Neal."

Piet walked to the companionway and entered the cabin. He didn't know which would be worse: Neal dead in the room or Neal alive in the room. It was complicated either way. If Neal was dead they could dump him overboard and disappear. Keep the boat, keep the money, and spend the rest of their lives fucking. If he was alive, well, he might have to be made dead.

He opened the door and saw that Neal was, in fact, alive: curled up on the floor in a fetal position.

"You okay?"

Neal nodded. "I think so."

Piet reached down and helped Neal to his feet, but Neal couldn't stand up straight. He was hunched over, holding his stomach. "I think I ruptured something."

That's when Piet noticed the duffel bags. "This the money?"

Neal nodded.

"How much is it?"

Neal winced. "Oh, I don't know. Twelve million? Fourteen? I didn't count it."

Piet nodded. Then he turned and slammed Neal headfirst into the wall, knocking him unconscious. Piet locked the door to the cabin, washed his face in the galley sink, and went out on deck and sat by Seo-yun.

"Is he okay?"

Piet looked at the ground and shook his head.

Seo-yun gasped. "Oh, my God. Oh, fuck." She burst into tears and let her face fall onto Piet's neck. He held her in his arms and let her cry. Piet decided he'd wait until she cried herself to sleep and then he'd dump Neal overboard.

Piet wanted to reassure her or say what needed to be said to make everything all right. But he just let her sob, feeling her warm body rise and fall against his. Of course feeling her that close turned him on. He couldn't help getting an erection. And then he received a faint transmission; it was her ass, talking to him. He concentrated, scrunching up his face, and tried to send a reply. Seo-yun shifted, wiped the tears from her eyes, and, as she moved, accidentally brushed her hand against his pants leg and felt his hard-on.

Seo-yun looked at him. "Now?"

He shrugged. "I can't help it. You turn me on."

She kissed him and he tasted the salt of her tears and a hint of white wine. Piet began undressing her. She let him pull her dress off. She unhooked her bra and shivered for a moment, her nipples hardening in the wind. "Poor Neal. He was really nice."

Piet nodded. "The nicest."

"I don't have a lot of friends at work and I thought we could be friends."

Piet kissed her again and said, "Why not come to Curaçao with me? We could live on the island and, you know, never worry about money again."

Seo-yun slid out of her panties. He couldn't read her expression. She seemed shocked but also kind of thrilled. Or maybe she was simply aroused. She looked at him and said, "You mean keep the money?"

He stepped out of his pants, letting his erection poke up into the air. "Live like royals and fuck all day long."

It is harder to tread water with a spear jutting out of your shoulder than you might think. That was the takeaway from this experience. But Bryan was glad that the local shark population hadn't sniffed out his wound. That was why he'd left the spear in—at least that way he wouldn't bleed to death or attract predators. He could simply fade into unconsciousness and drown. Then the scavengers could have at him.

It was almost a relief to be free of the money. Dying at sea was a suck-ass way to die, nobody was questioning that, but knowing that he didn't have to run or hide from anyone ever again, that felt good. Although he would've liked more time on the boat, even if just to spread some Camembert on a cracker and watch the sun set.

Bryan thought about the choices he'd made that led him to this point. Why had he gone into banking? Was it because his parents were wannabe bohemians? Was he rebelling? Did he become a banker because he never had cool clothes at school? His parents didn't care about the new sneakers or hoodies his friends wore. They told him that fads were ephemeral, tricks by evil marketing people to get you to replace things that were still good. As a teenager, Bryan had played his look off as style, as early neo-normcore. But his lack of teenage cool was the reason he couldn't get a date to the prom.

It's not that his parents were poor; they just had different priorities. Books. Art supplies. Nicaraguan charities. They were always pushing him to go to enrichment classes and study music or sculpture or something that he wasn't into. Naturally he discovered that the only way to break free of his upbringing was by earning as much money as he could. He could have gone into economics, maybe helped create a more just world. That was something he'd thought about in college, when being a social justice activist guaranteed he'd get laid. But how many economists had seven-figure salaries? Why should he be denied the trappings of wealth: the vacations, the two-hundred-dollar lunches, the safety and privilege of being on the side of the 1 percent? Wall Street had been a breeze, like running a casino. Easy money plucked from the wallets of rubes. It was fun.

He'd enjoyed planning the embezzlement, didn't feel bad about ripping off the company. He only felt guilty about Leighton. Bryan wondered if everything he'd ever done, every decision, had led up to this moment. Had he become a murderer because his parents wouldn't let him wear Nikes?

He saw something half submerged in a wave and kicked toward it. As he got closer he recognized it as a chunk of a surfboard drifting in the water. The board was painted with the words HAWAIIAN SOUL. He had no idea what a surfboard from Hawaii was doing in the Caribbean, but it might mean he was closer to land than he thought. Bryan clung to the board and laughed. He still had his new passport, some money in the bank. Things were looking up.

As any seismologist will tell you, the Cayman Trough runs in deep water along the ocean floor near where the Caribbean tectonic plate starts to crunch up against the North American tectonic plate. Squeezed in between these plates is the Gonâve microplate—the tuna salad in a tectonic sandwich bordered by the Septentrional-Oriente fault zone, which runs along the southern side of Cuba, and the Walton fault zone, which bends along the north coast of Jamaica. Occasionally the pressure of all these moving parts becomes too much and the Gonâve slips, creating an earthquake and sending powerful waves of energy up from the deep water and out across the Caribbean Sea. When the earthquakes are particularly strong, they can cause tsunamis, but even the milder slips and rumbles of the microplate can cause big waves. Rogue waves.

Bryan didn't know it, but as he clung to a piece of Hawaiian Soul and bobbed in the water, the Gonâve microplate slipped.

There was nothing wrong with the missionary position. Seo-yun didn't know why people disparaged it. She blamed those *Joy of Sex* books her grandparents hid in their bedside table. She'd looked through them when she was thirteen, and all those flip-flopping positions and funny angles just seemed like showing off. Done right, with some vigor and tenderness, the missionary position was a perfectly delightful way to have sex.

Piet had lowered the sail and let the boat drift. He told her he would take care of Neal's body, bury him at sea. Then they could set sail for Curaçao and she'd never have to talk to her fiancé again. She felt bad about Neal. But this was the chance of a lifetime. She could disappear. Start over. No one would know what happened. There were no witnesses; there was no evidence of anything. Not only could she break the rules, she could make her own rules. Maybe even live without rules. Fuck the rules. She could live an unbuttoned life. The more she thought about it, the more aroused she felt. Seo-yun began touching herself. She couldn't help it.

In the back of her mind she wondered if she had become mentally ill. Had the stress of her stupid wedding and the constant phone calls from her fiancé turned her into some kind of sex fiend?

Piet pushed her back on the bench and mounted her. Seo-yun lifted her legs and wrapped them around his body and felt him thrust into her. She heard the smack of their skin coming together, the dull slap of the waves against the hull. He reached a hand down and began tickling her clitoris as he fucked her. The song "One on One" by Hall and Oates started playing on the speakers and she smiled because it was appropriate, as if Bryan had cued it up just for her.

She could tell from the noises he was making that Piet was going to come soon. Seo-yun grabbed her breasts and gave her nipples a hard tweak. Her body began to shiver and convulse as her brain released serotonin and her breath caught. Her skin sparked with goose bumps and, as her body began to be rocked by undulating sensations, she felt something amazing happen;

it was unlike any orgasm she'd ever had before. Seo-yun felt her body become weightless, as if the boat were flying, defying gravity. It must have been what cosmonauts felt when they pierced the stratosphere and entered outer space. It was thrilling, unexpected. She felt his cock spasm as he ejaculated into her, both of them suspended together in the air.

As she came, Seo-yun opened her eyes and saw, right behind Piet's shoulder, a giant wall of water rising forty feet above the boat, like a sea monster emerging from the deep, blocking the sun; the power of the wave sucking the ship down into its embrace. She felt her stomach drop, as if she were on a roller coaster. Then the boat lurched and she and Piet fell off the bench onto the deck, still locked together, as the monster wave folded over them and swallowed the boat.

BECALMED

"I have to pee."

Chlöe shrugged. "So pee."

The jaunty jingle of a ringtone burst from the satellite phone in the cabin. Chlöe looked at Neal and walked across the deck toward the cabin, leaving him sitting there, one hand still strapped to the rail.

"I really have to pee."

Chlöe turned and kicked a plastic bucket in his direction. "Here."

The bucket banged into Neal's legs.

Chlöe went into the cabin and answered the sat phone. While her midnight call was a check-in to make sure she was alive, the daytime calls were a chance to say hello to friends, to get updates on the weather, her schedule, and any new corporate sponsors that might be jumping on the circumnavigational bandwagon. It was one of the things they realized as soon as she set sail: the longer she was at sea, the more corporate money came rolling in.

Of course more money meant more people wanting a piece of her. Photo ops with CEOs and celebrities had her sailing weeks off course, along with meet and greets, interviews with the press, anything to keep her in the news, keep the story trending. She was constantly taking time out of her day to produce photos and selfies and video clips and aspirational tweets to shovel into the insatiable orifice of social media. You could track her progress—follow her journey across the Pacific, through the Panama Canal, through the Caribbean—and get original content on Google Maps courtesy of the generous folks at the vitamin-packed sports drink company, or you could click on a link and be whisked to a special website that educated you on various topics like climate change, meteorology, famous women explorers, and the history of oceanic navigation, all courtesy of the Centre for Marine Science at the University of Queensland, sponsored by Foster's Lager—it's Australian for beer, mate.

A typical week might find her taking a detour to Honolulu to eat pineapple yogurt and drink Kona beer for the press, saying hi to young girls in a sailing club, then moving on to Maui for a private dinner and strategy session with corporate marketing execs who'd flown in from Silicon Valley.

When she got to Panama, a cruise line company arranged to sponsor her passage through the canal. All she had to do was be the guest of honor at the captain's table, shake a few hands, make a short speech, pose for some photos . . . which turned out to be six hours glad-handing two thousand sunburnt Americans while she tried not to catch the latest strain of norovirus.

As her number of online followers grew, so did the obligations required to get more and bigger donations. That was why she'd taken a weeklong detour through the Caribbean. She'd made promotional stops on Paradise Island and Turks and Caicos. Chlöe had to admit that there was nothing quite like docking in fancy marinas and being feted by big shots with corporate expense accounts. Taking a hot shower and drinking an ice-cold martini were two of her favorite things in life. Throw in a steak dinner and a couple bottles of Burgundy, and it was no surprise she found herself having a naughty in a luxury suite at the Atlantis resort. She wasn't sure what attracted her more, the allure of room service and soft cotton sheets, or the surprising handsomeness of the social media marketing manager who proclaimed himself an avid surfer. She had been horny, but whether it was for sex or a bubble bath, she couldn't say.

Chlöe wanted to be famous. And, to the extent that her name was in the news and her face was plastered on magazines and websites, she was. She had become the person they were selling: the daring adventurer taking on the world, the woman who'd lost her mother to breast cancer. She made sure she looked the part—strong and sexy and feminine as fuck.

But the problem with selling yourself as an adventurer was that you actually had to put in the long, lonely, physically punishing hours of adventuring. Right now it didn't look like she'd be going anywhere soon. The weather report wasn't encouraging. No wind in the forecast for at least twenty-four hours. Melbourne advised her to get some sleep, to let the boat drift with the current until the situation changed. The plan was for her to sail down the coast of South America, stopping in Rio and Montevideo for some press interviews, then turning east and crossing the Atlantic to Cape Town.

Chlöe lay down on her bed. Sleep was the biggest problem with solo sailing. Fatigue caused by sleep deprivation could lead you to do something stupid, like misread the water and end up dead. Oversleep and you could drift into the shipping lanes and get run over by a supertanker. Not to mention getting caught in a fast-moving storm or swamped by large swells. And then there were pirates. Not the Disney version of pirates; these were real steal-everything-you-got-and-dump-your-gang-raped-body-into-the-sea type of pirates.

Chlöe slept when she could, but unless she'd dropped anchor somewhere, she couldn't afford more than an hour at a time.

She looked out the cabin door and watched Neal contorting his body to piss in the bucket. He had his penis out, but it was a difficult angle and he was getting more urine on his clothes than in the bucket.

She was pretty sure he was a drug dealer. That much money in cash? It stood out like a dog's balls. What she'd do with him, well, she would have to sleep on it. She set her alarm for forty-five minutes and closed her eyes.

"My scalp is broiling. Do you have a hat or something?"

Chlöe shook her head.

Neal could feel the blisters sprouting. He tried to turn his head, anything to cast some shade on the side of his face, but the sky was cloudless, the sun directly above. It felt as if a waffle iron had been placed on his scalp.

She was standing, looking up at the sail, which was slapping lazily in the non-wind. "Looks like we're gonna sit here for a while."

"Which is why I need some kind of protection. I'm roasting. I could get skin cancer, you know."

Chlöe nodded. "It is hot. You're not lying about that."

There was something in her voice, an edge that stung Neal. "I'm not a liar. I'm not lying about anything."

He was going to continue to deny whatever accusations she might have concocted in her head, but the look on her face made him stop in midsentence. He sounded shrill, like someone who was over-denying it, who really was a big fat liar. Why didn't she believe him? Maybe he had omitted some details, but he was telling the truth about the money.

"Don't you have a business card or something? Some proof?"

Neal hung his head. *Why had he used his last card to send a hopeless message?* "One phone call to New York and you'd know I'm telling the truth."

"One phone call to New York and then the whole world knows I'm not traveling solo anymore."

"So I'm just going to sit here and cook?"

She nodded. "Looks that way."

He was about to say something else when she stripped off her shirt and stepped out of her shorts and underwear. She stood there for a moment, totally naked, and then dove off the boat into the water.

Neal felt an involuntary shudder rumble up his spine. His anxiety suddenly shifted into overdrive: the fear that a shark might devour her or she could get swept away, leaving him lashed to the rail. The nightmare vision of seagulls returned, swooping down on him, pecking out his eyes as he lay helpless, their beaks flashing red with his blood. He wondered where this fear came from. Birds, when they're not feeding on eyeballs, seemed nice enough. They flitted around and chirped. Some of them were beautiful. Bart would've said it was probably because he'd had his eyes pecked out by seagulls in a past life. Bart was spiritual like that.

Chlöe resurfaced, stroking calmly in the water a few yards from the boat.

"Are you sure it's safe?"

She whipped around, treading water by the boat. "What?"

"Aren't there sharks?"

She laughed. "I haven't seen any."

"It's the ones you don't see that are the problem."

She pulled herself onto the deck and reached for a towel. "You really aren't much of a sailor."

"I told you. First time on a boat and the big pole thing breaks."

"You were de-masted."

"That's the word."

She stood there drying her hair, water streaming off her skin. Neal couldn't help staring; the way the sunlight glinted off her breasts and the way the water dripped off her wild bush of pubic hair mesmerized him. Chlöe laughed. "You gonna crack a fat?"

Neal blinked and looked up at her face.

She translated: "Get a boner."

"No." Neal realized he said it too quickly. What if she took that as an insult? "I mean, you're very attractive, but I'm not that kind of guy."

She sat down opposite him, continuing to dry herself. "What kind of guy are you?"

"The kind that likes his own kind."

She smiled. "I see."

Neal wondered if this was some kind of game to her, if all this being tied up and questioned was her idea of foreplay. Maybe she was just kinky.

"So you've got nothing to worry about."

"I'm not particularly worried."

"Then why don't you untie me?"

"That"—she indicated the strap holding his wrist to the rail—"is what makes me not particularly worried."

He watched her slip back into her clothes, twist the cap off a bottle of water, and take a deep drink. Neal watched and realized that his throat was dry.

"Can I have a drink?"

She looked at him. "Why don't you give me a million dollars?"

"I can't. I told you. It's not my money."

"Right. And it's not your water, is it? That's how these things work. I would think a banker like yourself would understand the exchange of goods and services for money."

"I'll write an IOU."

She shook her head. "Cash only. No credit."

Neal sighed and slumped down against the rail. What was the point? Why not just pay her the money? Surely his boss would understand. Wouldn't he do the same thing if he were in Neal's shoes?

Chlöe looked at his scalp. "You're getting burned pretty badly. That's a shame. We've got a lot of skin cancer down under. Bad way to go."

Neal shook his head in anger. "Why are you doing this? Why can't you be nice?"

She smirked. "I see. You're one of those. Girls should be nice, is it?"

"People should help each other. Not fucking torture them." Neal realized he sounded angry. He didn't mean to, but he was miserable and he didn't know what else to do.

She studied him. "Is that what your investment bank does? Helps people? Helps people out of their homes, out of their pensions. Helps the fat cats get fatter."

"Why does everyone hate banks?"

She scoffed. "Are you serious?"

Why was everyone so quick to criticize? What would people do without banks to protect their savings? Give them loans? What would people do without a network of ATMs scattered around the world? Neal was sick and tired of people blaming all the problems in the world on Wall Street.

"We're the helping company, goddamn it. That's our motto." Neal thrashed against the strap, yanking on it until he cut his wrist. "We're motherfucking helpful. We're here to help motherfuckers."

She looked at him and laughed. "Oh, don't go off like a frog in a sock."

Neal stopped thrashing and took a deep breath. Yelling at her wasn't the way to show his gratitude. "I'm sorry. My brain is getting cooked."

For the first time since he'd been rescued, Chlöe looked sympathetic. "I'll tell you what. I'll sell you a hat for a million dollars and throw in a small bottle of water. What do you say?"

"Do you really think I stole the money? Do I look like a thief?"

She shrugged. Neal sighed. He didn't really have a choice. He could feel his skin being destroyed. Would it ever heal? Would he have to go on dates with a hat covering scar tissue?

"One hundred thousand for a hat and some water."

She laughed. "Really? You're going to bargain?"

"How big is the hat?"

She demonstrated with her hands. "It's a cap. An American baseball cap. It's got a nice visor, might be worth two million just for that."

Neal's head drooped. "Okay. Fine. A million dollars for some water and a hat."

Chlöe smiled. "Good choice." She came back with a pink baseball cap emblazoned with the words AROUND THE WORLD and stuck it on his head.

Chlöe went into the cabin and unzipped one of the duffel bags. Even though she'd sold him the hat and water for a million dollars, she decided that she'd take a million euros instead. She wasn't headed to the United States; it made more sense to take something easily converted. She figured he wouldn't discover the difference until she was long gone, and then what was he going to do? She'd saved his life.

She pulled out bundles of one-hundred-euro notes all banded together. Each bundle held ten thousand euros. She counted one hundred bundles and stowed them in the back of a cabinet, stacking boxes of Fantastic instant noodles in front of them. Fantastic was nice enough to be one of her sponsors and it had donated a year's supply of cup noodles in every flavor it made. She preferred the chicken flavor, so she pushed those to the front.

When she was done she took a coconut water out of the fridge and cracked it. Another sponsor. Cruelty-free coconut water. As if other companies picked coconuts that dropped off trees and conked people on the head. Chlöe couldn't have gotten this far without her sponsors, and they gave her a taste of the life she wanted.

Sponsors helped pay for the boat, they paid the salaries of her support team back in Melbourne. She thought she wanted to live like a movie star. If a movie star needed some new shoes, her shoe sponsor would deliver a crate. Same with cars, clothes, wine, whiskey, whatever you wanted. Of course she'd now learned that, from the outside, you think it's all free. Nobody tells you about the hidden costs, the responsibilities that come with being sponsored. It was nice at first, but lately, Chlöe felt it was just turning into a big fucking drag. It would be so much more fun to have a boatload of money and sponsor herself.

The unmistakable funk of thick urine stung his nostrils. Why had she made him piss in a bucket? You try hitting the target with one hand while you're lashed to a rail.

Neal shifted, trying to keep the wet part of his pants from sticking to his skin. In some small way he was glad that he'd pissed all over the place. She was the one who'd tied him up; she could enjoy the smell too. Besides, what had he done to deserve any of this? He gave her a million bucks for a trucker hat. What more could she want?

He tugged on the plastic tie holding his hand to the boat rail, jerking it up and down, trying to create some slack. The more he pulled the angrier he got, until he was yanking on it as hard as he could, hoping to snap the plastic or the boat rail or even his wrist bone. He stopped when he felt the plastic bite deep into his skin. He winced as the salt air settled in the cut, stinging him back to his senses.

Resistance is futile. Isn't that what they said on *Star Trek*?

He watched as Chlöe emerged from the cabin. She'd obviously taken one of the many short naps he'd seen her take, but instead of looking refreshed, she looked even more exhausted. Neal wondered if she might fall asleep on the deck. She kept a folding knife clipped to her shorts; would it be that difficult to knock her down, take the knife, and cut himself free? But then what? Tie her up and convince her he was a good guy?

Chlöe stood over him and wrinkled her nose. "Christ, you stink."

"Well, if you'd just let me use your toilet . . ."

Before he could finish his thought, she dipped the plastic bucket into the sea and hurled water at him.

Neal spluttered. "What the fuck?"

"You should be thanking me."

Neal blinked his eyes, trying to keep the salt water from burning them. "Thanks."

Chlöe smiled. "Sarcasm is the last refuge of scoundrels."

Neal glowered. "I'm not a scoundrel."

"We'll see about that. Because if you ask me, a man floating around the ocean with all this cash looks like he might be a scoundrel. Maybe a pirate. A rogue at the very least."

Neal shook his head. "I told you I work for an investment firm."

Chlöe laughed. "And this is some new version of offshore banking."

Neal felt his face flush in frustration. "One of my colleagues died trying to get this money. Or at least I think she died." As he said the words he was overcome with a feeling of real sadness. He assumed Seo-yun was dead and he felt terrible about it.

"You're just going to take the money back to the bank?"

"It's their money."

Chlöe shook her head. "Seems like a waste to me."

Neal didn't say anything.

"Is there a reward?"

Neal blinked. "Reward for what?"

"For getting you and this money safely back on land."

"I don't think so."

"A finder's fee? Maybe twenty percent."

Neal shook his head. "I can't authorize anything like that."

Chlöe looked at him for a long time without saying anything. Then she said, "That's too bad."

When did the idea sneak up on her? Was it when she first opened the duffel bags? Was it when she decided that he was probably telling the truth, or some version of the truth, and wasn't a drug dealer or an international criminal? He was probably what he said he was. A guy who worked for a bank. The same bank that helped tank the global economy. Chlöe laughed to herself. What was she trying to do? Justify what she was thinking? Australia skated through the financial meltdown. She wasn't affected by it. Besides, were the actions of a corporation, no matter how crook, justification for murder?

Chlöe put the kettle on. She ripped the lids off two cups of Fantastic noodles and waited for the water to boil. She wished she'd rescued a handsome big wave surfer, a sun-kissed ocean god, someone with long hair and an incredible body, someone who would fuck the loneliness right out of her. But no, instead of Eddie Aikau or John John Florence, she rescued gay Neal from accounting.

She carefully poured hot water into the cups of noodles and then closed the lids. She sat back and waited for the noodle magic to happen. There were so many things she could do with that money. The life she could make for herself. It was wrong, of course, completely wrong. But if, for the sake of argument, this bloke were to vanish on the high seas, it's not as if anyone would ever know.

Chlöe carried the noodle cups out onto the deck and handed one to Neal. He took it with one hand. "This smells delicious."

"Be careful, it's hot."

"It'd be easier to eat with both hands." Neal looked at her. Chlöe stared back at him, considering various possible comebacks, but if she were being honest with herself, she was too fucking tired to think of anything. He must've sensed it, because he squirmed and said, "Not that I'm complaining. Thank you for sharing your food with me."

"Well, we can't have you starving to death. Wouldn't be good for the brand."

With that, Chlöe pointed up at the sail and all the corporate logos.

Neal slurped his soup, taking in a big ball of noodles, his face twisting as he attempted to keep from burning the inside of his mouth. Chlöe watched him. A normal person would've spit the hot soup out, but a starving man will suffer second-degree burns for a mouthful of delicious ramen. She realized that if he started choking, she wouldn't apply the Heimlich or try to save him. She'd just go down in the galley and make a cup of tea while he asphyxiated.

Chlöe scooped up a tangle of noodles with her chopsticks and blew on them. Perhaps that was the way to do it. An accident. He choked. He drowned. He was leaning over the side of the boat washing his hair when a great white came up and decapitated him.

Chlöe chewed on her noodles. Turning the banker into shark biscuit made the most sense.

And that's when she knew what she was going to do.

"When I get back to New York, I think I'll start over." Neal looked up at Chlöe. She didn't seem that interested; she seemed preoccupied. "I'll start dating again."

Chlöe nodded. "That's nice."

"Do you have someone?"

"What? Like a boyfriend?"

"Yeah. A significant other."

"Does someone with a boyfriend decide to spend a year on a boat?"

Neal had to admit that someone who was spending a year alone at sea probably didn't have a boyfriend. He followed her gaze up to some streamers on top of the mast. They were starting to twitch a little. "Looks like wind."

She nodded. "Weather report says we should have good sailing by the afternoon."

"Where are you taking me?"

She gave him a smirk. "I'm not taking you to fucking New York." She cranked a rope and tightened the sail. "And I'm not taking you to Grand Cayman."

Neal didn't know why she was in such a bad mood. "It doesn't matter. Anywhere will do."

"Good. Because I was thinking maybe Suriname."

Neal realized he didn't know where Suriname was. "What? Where's that?"

"In between Guyana and French Guyana."

"Do they have an airport there?"

She looked at him as if he was a complete moron. "I reckon they have airports everywhere nowadays."

Neal decided that maybe he would sign up for a geography class at the New School. He should know where those countries are. If the New School didn't have a class, maybe he could go to a travel bookstore and read up on places. Maybe he should travel more. Bart had always wanted to take one of those gay cruises, a naked gay cruise, but Neal didn't know if he could do it; he felt too paunchy, too pasty to be naked on a boat with a bunch of buffed and burnished men. Although now that he thought of it, there were probably loads of men just like him. Maybe he should go on a naked gay cruise.

"Have you ever been on a cruise?"

"Like a ship?"

Neal nodded. "Yeah. One of those fancy ones."

Chlöe shook her head. "I hear they're heaps of fun, but it's out of my price range."

"I think I'll go on one when I get back. It'd be a good place to meet someone."

The wind picked up and the boat began to move. Chlöe turned and looked at him. "You sound awfully desperate to meet someone."

He realized she was probably right, but before he could catch himself he said, "I'm lonely." But then he added, "Or I was lonely. Now I think I'll be okay."

She laughed. "I'll alert the press."

He laughed with her. "It's weird, but I'm starting to feel good again."

"Ready for dessert?"

"Sure."

He watched as she locked the tiller into a strap and walked into the cabin. Neal relaxed. Even though having his arm strapped to the rail was uncomfortable, it was a small price to pay to keep from starving to death. And soon enough he'd be back home, eating at some trendy new place, having poached halibut with a side of sautéed spinach. Perhaps he'd indulge in a cocktail, maybe a boulevardier. After dinner he would stroll back to his apartment and lie on his couch. There was plenty of room to spread out on. Everything was possible. The CEO would probably give him a bonus, and then he could take a proper vacation. A naked gay cruise sounded like just the thing.

Chlöe came out of the cabin carrying a couple of smoothies. She handed one to him. "Protein shake. Not the best-tasting item in the galley, but it'll give you some energy."

Neal took it with his free hand. "Thanks." He took a taste and winced. "This is terrible."

Chlöe nodded. "Yeah. But it's all protein and vitamins. I just chug them." And with that she raised hers to her lips and slugged it down. Neal drank the shake as quickly as he could, silently vowing never to have another one again.

Chlöe held the tiller steady, letting the sail catch some wind, feeling the boat moving, picking up speed. She was about a hundred miles off the coast of Venezuela heading southeast. Her original plan—putting in promotional stops in Rio de Janeiro, São Paulo, Montevideo, and Buenos Aires—was about to change.

She looked over at Neal. He was unconscious, his head lolling from side to side with the swells. He fucking should be out; Chlöe had crunched up seven Vicodin and mixed them into his protein shake. She was glad he finally conked. If he'd continued going on and on about his miserable love life, she might've just beaten him with a hammer. But the drugs eventually kicked in. That was one consolation. He might be about to die, but he wasn't going to feel any pain, which made her feel a bit better, as if she was a humane murderer. It reminded her of the time she had to euthanize her dog. It was sad, but he had doggie cancer and it ended his pain.

The idea of killing someone had never really occurred to her. Not seriously. Sure, she'd imagined blowing away some would-be rapist or taking a hatchet to a sexist asshole at the Melbourne Yacht Club, but she'd never really thought she'd find herself in a situation where homicide was justifiable. Not that it was legally justifiable or even ethically justifiable, and yet she figured almost anyone in her position would do the same. She would never be able to have money like this, ever, no matter how famous she was, no matter how many times she circled the Earth in a small boat. She could circle the moon and they wouldn't pay her this much.

And it was so easy. For all anyone would ever know, the gay accountant went down with his ship.

It was time. The sun was setting, the wind was strong, and she could start putting some distance between herself and this part of the world.

She crouched beside Neal and pulled out her folding knife. One quick slice of the strap and Neal's right arm was free. Chlöe lifted him up and sat him on the edge of the boat. She didn't want to dwell on it, didn't want to hesitate or change her mind. This was a once-in-a-lifetime opportunity. She gave him a gentle push and Neal tumbled into the water.

She immediately regretted it. She threw the sailboat into a sharp turn and began to drop the sail. She circled back to the spot where he'd gone in but there was no sign of him. No bubbles, nothing. He'd sunk into the sea without a trace.

It was twilight. The sky shifted from pale blue to indigo, the water turned black. The wind was picking up and waves began to bang against the hull as she let the boat drift. It was too late for Neal.

Chlöe sat down on the deck and began to sob.

Orestes Pérez pulled on the rope. It was heavy, which was good, because it meant that there would be something in the trap. With any luck it might be a few lobsters, maybe a couple of stone crabs, hopefully not a clump of kelp. His small boat rocked back and forth as he pulled. When the trap was near the surface he stopped and rested. It was hot out, and he was sweating like a roasting pig, the salty perspiration burning his eyes, soaking through his tank top. And he was hungry. He'd been dancing last night at the bar, which meant that this morning he hadn't had an appetite. He'd knocked back a cup of sweet black coffee and then he was out on the water. His plan was to work the traps quickly and get back to shore by lunchtime. Then he could spend the rest of the day in his hammock.

Luckily the sea was smooth and he could check his traps without too much effort. He hauled the trap out of the water and dumped the contents on the floor of the boat: five big lobsters and a mature stone crab. It was a small miracle. He quickly put the crustaceans into a bucket of seawater, baited the trap, and chucked it back in. Orestes grinned. The lobsters were all good-size. They would bring a lot of money from the chef at the resort.

There were other traps to check, but he decided not to push his luck. Also his hangover was starting to get the better of him. He could come check the other traps tomorrow.

As he set a float on the trapline, he saw a bottle bobbing on the surface. It drifted over and banged against the hull of the boat, knocking on the wood as if it wanted to come aboard. Orestes didn't believe in ghosts, but he didn't not believe in them either, so he fished the bottle out of the water. No wine. Just a small piece of paper with some writing on it. He couldn't read English, so he didn't know that the card was from Neal Nathanson, employee of a prestigious Wall Street investment bank. But the bottle looked promising. The cap had a tight seal. A good glass bottle was always useful.

Orestes put the bottle on the floor of the boat next to his bucket of lobsters and began rowing toward shore. When he got close to the beach he jumped out and dragged his boat up onto the sand.

He was surprised to see Yanet sitting in the shade of some coconut palms. She stood to greet him and gave him a coconut with a straw in it. Orestes smiled.

Yanet looked into the bucket and her eyes widened.

Orestes fell in love easily—some people said that was his downfall—but how could he resist Yanet? He offered to make her lunch right there on the beach. The biggest, fattest lobster. He would sell the others to the resort.

Quickly gathering some small pieces of wood and some twigs for kindling, he began building a fire. He had a small metal grate that he carried in his boat for alfresco lunches on the beach and put that over the wood. Using one of the sticks, he carefully pulled the paper from inside the bottle and struck a match. It caught fire quickly and Orestes used it to ignite the kindling.

While the fire got going, he took his knife and split the biggest lobster down the middle, cleaned the lungs and guts out of it, rinsed it in the sea, and laid it on the metal grate to roast.

Orestes and Yanet didn't know that the business card was the only remaining evidence of what had happened to Neal Nathanson. They didn't know that, as far as anyone could tell, he and his colleague Seo-yun Kim had vanished without a trace. It didn't concern them. They were falling in love.

POSEIDON

As the ferry neared Skiathos, Cuffy Ebanks hung his head over the side and looked at the water. It was the same water that Odysseus had sailed, water that had seen the Greek fleet battle Xerxes and his invading Persian army, a sea that had endured the best and worst of human activity for a few thousand years, and yet it was immaculate: epic blue and crystalline. The same history had happened on land, but had left scars: ruins and wastelands. Cuffy had a lot of respect for the power of the ocean. The sea had been good to him, had saved his life, and now that he was in Poseidon's backyard, he felt a surge of bittersweet regret mixed with a kind of life-affirming euphoria.

A bird swooped overhead, and he looked up and saw the city, a pile of white boxes with orange roofs lining a perfect crescent beach.

The gangplank dropped and Cuffy disembarked with the other tourists. He wandered the front street, past a string of restaurants and cafés facing the water. He stopped at a kiosk offering tours to visit the locations from the movie *Mamma Mia!* Cuffy hadn't seen the film but knew it was based on the songs of palindromic supergroup ABBA. Was it weird that a Swedish pop group would be an economic boon for a small

Greek island? Was this the globalization everyone was talking about?

The town was beautiful and, like all the other Greek islands he'd been to, riddled with quirky footpaths and stairs that were painted white, as if they were meant to create trompe l'oeil flagstones. He didn't understand why.

Cuffy found a café and sat at a table. Unlike the other tourists, he didn't check for Wi-Fi. He had no email, no social media, no internet presence of any kind. Not that he'd become antitechnology; he had a smartphone that he used to look up information, to book hotels and flights.

An espresso sounded like a good idea, but he ordered a Fix instead. He liked the idea of a beer named Fix, even if he was drinking before lunch. Or maybe he was just blending in; beer before noon might be just the thing on Skiathos, a place the guidebooks called the "most cosmopolitan island in the Northern Sporades."

He had a couple of hours before he could check in at his hotel, so after he finished his beer, he ordered another one. And after that, a third to go with the grilled octopus and Greek salad. It had taken him almost two years to get here, and still he wasn't sure if he was on the right track or not. It wouldn't be the first trail he'd followed to a dead end.

Cuffy found the hotel easily enough. He meandered up several flights of winding stairs toward the top of the town, following nicely painted signs that said HOTEL THALIA in a Hellenic-style font. The tourist shops selling T-shirts and bottles of olive oil were closer to the harbor, and as he climbed farther up the hill, it became more residential. There were little cafés, greengrocers, bakeries, bookstores, and scooter repair shops mixed in with homes and apartments. He could see the appeal of a place like this.

The Thalia was one of those boutique hotels—an austere modern design imposed on an old building—and boasted a swimming pool and cocktail bar. It had only recently opened and was the second hotel on the island to be awarded four stars.

An athletic woman with a deep tan and an Australian accent greeted him from behind the front desk when he walked into the lobby. "Checking in?"

"Yes."

He handed over his passport. She looked at it and began typing on an iPad. "Mr. Ebanks. Right. Staying for three nights."

"Correct."

She looked at the passport, then at Cuffy. "You're British? You don't have an accent."

"I'm from the Cayman Islands. We're part of the Commonwealth, so . . . you know . . . UK passports."

She handed his passport back and their eyes met.

Cuffy smiled at her. "You're the sailor, right? Sailed around the world all by yourself."

She nodded. "Wouldn't want to do that again."

"I imagine it was quite an adventure."

The room was nice, austere but surprisingly comfortable, with an intentionally minimal and elegant vibe. Cuffy was pleased to see a typewriter from the 1960s next to a Nespresso machine.

He dumped his backpack on a chair and went to the window. His room had a beautiful view of the bay and a couple of smaller islands in the distance. It was stunning. Even with the economic crisis Greece was suffering, the property must have been expensive.

He sat on the bed and read the brochure he'd picked up in the lobby. Hotel Thalia had opened only six months ago after a multimillion-dollar renovation. He was surprised that the brochure didn't mention the owner, the famous sailor. Perhaps she wanted to be left alone. He couldn't help noticing that her eyes had a haunted look: the look of someone who didn't sleep well, someone who was weighed down by guilt and grief and regret; they were the eyes of a murderer. It was the same look he saw in the mirror every morning.

Chlöe loved her hotel. It was everything she'd hoped it would be. Only instead of it being in Melbourne, where she could be close to her family and friends, it was in Greece. She could have built it at home, but she wasn't comfortable in Australia anymore, didn't like who she was, the woman who sailed around the world. She didn't like being a role model or an example for other women. Didn't want to make up lies about where she got the money.

If she was being honest, she didn't like herself.

At first there had been mood swings. Then came the panic attacks—heart pounding, cold sweat, adrenal glands in overdrive—the feeling-that-you're-dying kind of panic attacks. She'd seen a doctor but got a clean bill of health. Chlöe had tried talking to a psychiatrist but, without revealing her big secret, it didn't really help. She had a prescription for antianxiety meds, but they just made her feel weird. Much better was a bottle or two of wine or a few cocktails. People say self-medicating is bad. As far as she was concerned, those people could go fuck themselves. Dealing with a hangover, or kicking some one-night stand out of your bed, was way easier than trying to think through a pharma fog.

She tried confessing to a priest, but when it came time to unburden her soul she couldn't do it. There were selfless attempts at making amends. For a brief while she was an ambassador for the Indigenous Literacy Foundation, doing speeches and meet and greets to raise money to bring books and classes to underserved Aboriginal populations. She volunteered at homeless shelters and gave sailing lessons to poor children. And when all this charitable work started to make her feel like a fraud, she traveled to Nepal to learn meditation from a Buddhist monk. Meditation didn't help. Her mind was restless, she couldn't sit still, so she roamed. People back home thought she'd caught the travel bug, as if that were some kind of virus that compelled you to drift from city to city, mountains to seaside. She began to feel fatalistic, preferring dangerous forms of transportation, always hoping the motorcycle would crash, the ferry would sink, the bus would run off the road.

It was during her travels that she discovered Skiathos. It was beautiful, quiet, and best of all, she wasn't a celebrity here; no one cared about her exploits. She could start over. Be a better her, whatever that meant.

And that's what she did.

He'd spent the day idling: doing some reading and taking short walks around the city, coming back and seeing that she was still working. He wasn't sure how to approach her or what to say to break the ice. She probably didn't want to talk about it. Why would she? But as the sun began to fade, he saw her say something to the night clerk, grab her purse, and head out.

He followed her.

He kept her in his sight as she left the hotel and turned the corner, walking up several flights of stairs, turning to the right, up another flight, then a left, until she entered a small church tucked between what looked like apartment buildings. The church was tiny, maybe big enough for five people, freshly whitewashed with cobalt paint on the door and window trim. The door hung open, and Cuffy watched as she lit a candle and bent her head in prayer. He didn't want her to see him when she came out, so he walked to the end of an alley, where he found a white cat curled in a shaft of sunlight, trying to catch the last rays before night. Cuffy scratched its head and the cat began to purr.

He heard her footsteps echo on the stairs going down and he followed her. She was walking faster now, downhill, gliding through a series of careening switchbacks through the alleys and small footpaths between houses. He tried to keep up, losing her at one point and having to sprint along an alley to catch a glimpse of her going down another set of steps.

He eventually found her outside a small taverna—the sign said TAVERNA MESOGIA—sitting alone at a table for two. Trying to be as casual as he could, Cuffy sauntered up to her. "Hey. Is this place good?"

She looked up at him. "Mr. Ebanks. Why, yes, this place is ace. Best food on the island."

Cuffy hesitated. "Mind if I join you?"

She seemed startled by the request. "Um, well, I don't see why not."

Cuffy pulled out a chair and sat across from her.

The taverna spilled into the alley, as if the throughway was just another part of the restaurant. A strand of lights entwined in the grapevine blinked on, and a young waiter brought a red metal pitcher of white wine and plonked it on the blue-checked tablecloth.

She poured the wine into two tumblers. Cuffy took his and said, "Cheers." She smiled at him and touched her glass against his. "*Yamas.*"

Cuffy took a sip. The wine was delicious. "This is excellent. Is it local?"

She shook her head. "I believe it's from Santorini."

The waiter came over to take their order. Cuffy shrugged and looked at her. "This is your place, why don't you order? I'll put my life in your hands."

She smiled. "Little-known fact, this is one of the best restaurants in the world. They grill everything on charcoal."

Cuffy thought he detected a twitch in her smile, a subconscious reveal. He'd come to the island with a question for her, but was unsure how to ask it. He was equally unsure what would happen if he did. He took a long, deep sip of wine and watched as she ordered what seemed like an excessive amount of food for both of them.

"You must be hungry."

She looked at him. "Aren't you?"

The food never stopped coming: a Greek salad, octopus boiled in vinegar, dolmas, large beans stewed in tomato sauce, fried zucchini croquettes, eggplant in various forms, saganaki, calamari grilled over coals, and then lamb baked with lemons. Every bite he put in his mouth was amazing, as sensual and life affirming as anything he'd ever experienced. And the wine didn't stop. As soon as they finished one red metal pitcher, another would take its place.

Cuffy felt sated. They were both full of wine and food, and the dread he was feeling lifted. Another pitcher arrived and she began filling their glasses.

"Thank you."

"Thanks for the company."

Cuffy looked at her, their eyes locking. He realized that this was probably the best, maybe only moment to ask her the question that had been haunting him for two years. "I hope this isn't too forward of me, but there's something I want to ask you."

"A personal question?"

He nodded. "Yes."

She smiled. "As long as it's not about sailing."

He smiled back at her and said, "I know this is going to sound strange. Out of left field really, but I need to know."

She looked slightly worried. "Okay."

"I'm not judging in any way. I'm looking for advice, really." He took a sip of wine, then said, "How do you live with yourself?"

She blinked. "I'm not sure I follow."

"I thought that the money had sunk with the boat. You know, boat's gone, money's gone. Everyone's dead. But then I thought, well, maybe there was a rescue. So I looked into what other boats were out there at the time. Maritime records are sketchy, but you were out there."

She hesitated, then said, "It's a big ocean."

He could see she was getting agitated, as if she was about to get up and walk off, so he tried to reassure her. "Look, I'm not a policeman. I don't want the money. I'm not going to cause you any trouble." He paused. "You don't have to say anything. I already know."

She glanced over her shoulder, as if to make sure they were alone. "What do you know?"

"Most people would do what you did."

She seemed to recognize something in his expression. "How would you know?"

Cuffy locked eyes with her. "Kill or be killed. That's what I told myself anyway."

She let out a sigh and hung her head. "I'm so fucking tired."

"I'm just trying to figure out what happened. To close the loop, I guess."

She blinked back tears and then he saw the realization form on her face. "You're the embezzler."

"Yes."

She took a deep breath. "Neal said you'd been killed by a speargun."

The mention of the speargun made Cuffy reach for his shoulder. "I eventually washed up."

She raised her glass, took a sip. "I imagine you had quite a ride."

He didn't reply. It had been quite a ride. But then again, the ride wasn't over. Finally he asked, "So Neal was alive?" Tears spurted out of her eyes. Cuffy handed her his napkin and said, "Never mind."

She blew her nose and tried to compose herself.

He sighed. "You did some nice things with the money. The hotel is really lovely."

"Thanks." And then she added, "Consider it your home away from home. No charge. Stay as long as you like."

"Wouldn't that be awkward?"

She shrugged. "Fuck if I know. I can't believe I'm saying this, but I'm happy to have someone to share this thing with. It's such a burden."

"I know."

Another red metal pitcher of wine appeared at the table. She leaned in and spoke softly. "So? What do we murderers do?"

"I wish I had an answer for that."

"I've been praying. Every day."

"Does it make you feel better?"

She shook her head. "I feel like shit after I go to church."

He refilled their glasses and said, "I avoid spirituality. There's no good end for us when you start down that road."

Her face reddened. Her lips trembled. Finally she said, "Fuck."

They sat there in silence, sipping the delicious white wine from Santorini, feeling the breeze off the ocean drift through the alley, listening to the sounds of the people around them, smelling the food from the taverna. The world around them was fully alive, saturated. Cuffy felt that he was part of the continuum of history, here in this alley—a piece of the pulse of humanity. For the first time in his life he felt connected instead of disconnected.

"I see why you like this place."

A group of tourists walked past them. Laminated cards from a cruise ship spun on lanyards around their necks.

Chlöe wiped some mucus from her nose. "I can't believe I did it. You know? Fucking money." He handed her another napkin. "That's the thing, right? You always think, *If I just had a few million dollars everything would be great,* and then . . . you get the money and . . . you know."

"Everything is shit."

He couldn't tell if she was sad about having to relive it or relieved to have someone who understood, but seeing her cry brought tears to his eyes, and he found himself sobbing softly with her. Everything was shit and everything was beautiful. They were both haunted by the dead. So were these streets, so was this island, and yet it didn't stop the place from brimming with life. Cuffy thought about his parents—the way people carried the dead with them, how that fueled their lust for life—and for the first time in a long time he felt safe: linked to the past, looking to the future, happy in the moment.

Cuffy raised his glass:

"Everything is shit and everything is beautiful."

ACKNOWLEDGMENTS

I am deeply indebted to my editor, Corinna Barsan, for her intelligence, enthusiasm, generosity, and humor.

Big ups and undying gratitude to the crew at Grove Atlantic: Captain Morgan Entrekin, Judy Hottenson, Deb Seager, Justina Batchelor, Zachary Pace, Allison Malecha, Gretchen Mergenthaler, and Julia Berner-Tobin. Thanks to Nancy Tan and Susan Gamer for eyeballing the copy. Bart Heideman at Uncanny Design; and Martin Rusch for the photograph. And to Mary Evans, Julia Kardon, and Brian Lipson for taking care of business.

Special thanks to Indy Flore, Jamison Stoltz, JoAnn Chaney, Liska Jacobs, David L. Ulin, Diana Faust, and Olivia Taylor Smith for their thoughtful comments on the manuscript and to Mara Amster, Laura Grey-Street, and Gary Dop at Randolph College for giving me some space to write in.

And a shout-out to my friends and family who encourage this work in innumerable ways: Tod Goldberg, Agam Patel, Bruce and Cynthia Faust, Jim Peterson, Katie and Amy at Society of the Spectacle, Alex Wolff, Norman B, and Jules Haskell Smith.

GRA
0
BASE CO BIG I 2? ???

EAGLE VALLEY LIBRARY DISTRICT
P.O. BOX 240 600 BROADWAY
EAGLE, CO 81631 / 328-8800